D0425080

TOP SOLDIER

Center Point
Large Print

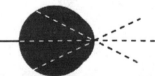

**This Large Print Book carries the
Seal of Approval of N.A.V.H.**

TOP SOLDIER

Johnny D. Boggs

CENTER POINT LARGE PRINT
THORNDIKE, MAINE

This Circle **Ṽ** Western is published by
Center Point Large Print in the year 2016 in
co-operation with Golden West Literary Agency.

Copyright © 2016 by Johnny D. Boggs.

All rights reserved.

June, 2016
First Edition

Printed in the United States of America
on permanent paper.
Set in 16-point Times New Roman type.

ISBN: 978-1-68324-010-5

Library of Congress Cataloging-in-Publication Data

Names: Boggs, Johnny D.
Title: Top soldier / Johnny D. Boggs.
Description: First edition. | Thorndike, Maine : Center Point Large Print,
2016. | Series: A Circle V western
Identifiers: LCCN 2016004479 | ISBN 9781683240105
Subjects: LCSH: United States—History—Civil War, 1861–1865—
Veterans—Fiction. | Indians of North America—Texas—Fiction. |
Texas—Fiction. | Large type books. | GSAFD: Western stories.
Classification: LCC PS3552.O4375 T67 2016 | DDC 813/.54—dc23
LC record available at https://lccn.loc.gov/2016004479

For Henry T. Price,
my toughest, favorite,
and best college professor

PROLOGUE

Papa wore the gray.

That is not a saying you hear from many middle-aged men living in Leechburg, Pennsylvania, especially these days, what with the 40th anniversary of the Battle of Gettysburg, roughly two hundred miles to the southeast, fast approaching. Most of the Irish and the Germans working with me for the Paulton Coal Mining Company are descendants of Yankees, and a few old-timers even wore the blue. As far as I know, I am the lone Southerner.

Let me explain. William Lee Braden, my father, was no Secessionist, no slave owner, and I'm still not certain why he even rode off in the fall of 1861 to join his brother in Harrisburg to fight for the Confederacy.

No, that's not right. Papa and my uncle were not fighting for the Confederacy.

They fought for Texas.

Like most Jack County men, when the polls opened in Jacksboro on February 23, 1861, Papa rode the twelve miles up Lost Creek to cast his vote against the Secession Ordinance. Mr. W.L. Braden not only voted, he even wrote—*For the Union forever*—next to his signature. Papa had never been that vocal about anything, but even as the cry for Secession reached a furor across the Lone Star State, you would find several pockets and communities in northern Texas, like Jack County, filled with men who followed Sam Houston—some literally as far back as the Republic years and the Battle of San Jacinto; others, as in Papa's case, figuratively. They were followers of Andrew Jackson, loyal to the Stars and Stripes, for the moment anyway. Jack County voted 76–14 to stay in the Union.

Which proved to be a forlorn hope.

Sam Houston refused to take the oath to the Confederate States of America, got kicked out as governor, and would be dead in a couple of years. A few other Texas counties voted not to join the Confederacy, but the public overwhelmingly supported the movement to withdraw from the Union, which everyone knew meant war. So when my uncle, Jacob Braden, wrote to Papa, asking him to join what became known as Hood's Texas Brigade, my father rode off with a half dozen other Jack County men, a few who had voted to leave the Union, but many who wanted to stay—most wanted nothing to do with the war fast approaching.

Well, that's another thing about Texans, then and today. They're loyal to neighbors, to family, to the land they call home. First and foremost, Papa and the citizens of Jack County considered themselves Texans, which is why Papa wore that Confederate uniform.

Unlike more than a few of my friends' fathers, Papa would return some four years later. He would come home to Texas, to Mama and me. He would return with scars from two bullet wounds and another from a bayonet. He would be credited with saving his brother's life, and he would bring back a medal that he had been given, personally, by General John Bell Hood.

Yet, for a time, I thought Papa a coward.

PART I
1861–1866

CHAPTER ONE

I was only a button when the war broke out, merely five years old, so any recollection of those years is nothing more than a snatch of memories, some clear, most blurred by other events.

Here's what I know of my family.

Papa was born in Harrisburg, way down in South Texas near Houston. Four years after Papa entered this world, Uncle Jake was born there, too. Two sons of a wealthy planter, but Papa developed a case of wanderlust. Jacob Braden? He liked the balls and the belles and the money and ease of life that King Cotton gave him. Papa, on the other hand, wanted something different, something he could make for himself, not just have given to him because he was Jonathan James Braden's son. So upon turning eighteen, Papa bid good bye and rode to San Antonio. Austin. Then Dallas.

His travels and wayfaring ways always gave me pause, for I knew Uncle Jake as the wild and reckless one, but Papa? By the time I was of an age to notice such things, Papa seemed like an old man.

The War for the Southern Confederacy changed them both.

Rooted to the land of cheap grass, reddish clay, shale, and sandstone, Papa worked sunup to sundown, uttering as few sentences as possible. He never said grace—leaving that job to Mama— but he always made sure we left at least one biscuit or piece of cornbread on the table after supper, in case some visitor called. As if anyone would ride out to our hardscrabble place, roughly one mile before Lost Creek flowed into the West Fork of the Trinity River.

We had a real house, though, made of log and stone. When he and Mama first moved to Jack County, Papa had suggested that they start off with nothing more than a dugout, but Mama would hear none of that.

"The only time I expect to have dirt over my head, Wil," she said, "is when I'm dead."

They had first met in Dallas. Papa had met Martha Jane Pierce, who had come with her folks and siblings from North Carolina. As Mama said, she and Papa got into a "whirl" in Dallas. Martha's father and uncle and their oldest sons had gone off to help settle what originally was land designated for something called the Texan Emigration and Land Company. They had set out with pack saddles, called "kayaks," and coffee pots and tin cups hanging from rawhide straps around the necks of their mules.

By the time the Pierces had returned to Dallas to fetch the women and children, Grandpa Adair realized there would be no getting rid of William Braden. Even before the Pierce clan had reached

Tarrant County, with their wagons and milch cows and chickens and packs of Carolina hounds, she and Papa were betrothed. They married in Fort Worth, and Papa joined the Pierces as they journeyed west to the land they had staked for themselves. That was 1855. I came along a year later.

They gave me Mama's maiden name. Pierce. Pierce Jonathan Braden.

By the winter of 1858, Grandpa and Grandma Pierce had given up, beaten by the land, the sun, and the Indians. Northwest Texas proved a whole lot different than the piney woods of Carolina. Dry, hilly, and hard, populated along the creeks and rivers with mesquites, scrubby oaks, pecan, elm, and walnut trees, and cottonwoods, but mostly a land of tough, rolling hills and that vast, almost endless, Texas sky.

And Indians. Closest were the Tonkawas, always friendly to the whites, but the Comanches to the west and Kiowas to the north were not friendly at all.

One of my uncles, Charles Pierce, I never got to know. Along West Keechi Creek in the spring of 1858, Comanches killed him and three of his dogs that he had taken along hunting. They took his horse, and his scalp.

My guess is that the loss of Charles sent Grandpa and Grandma south to Austin, which was civilized. They begged Mama to come with them, and Papa and me, too, but Papa had grown stubborn, and Mama . . . maybe even more so.

Looking back, I guess you couldn't blame the Indians, although everyone I knew in those days most certainly did blame them. They were our enemies—they hated us; we hated them—much like it would be with the Yankees. Still, we had run off the buffalo, replacing those shaggy beasts with cattle on what had once been Indian land.

Jack County, you see, was turning into cow country, with open range for anyone with half a mind to make that kind of living. That appealed to Papa. He delivered cattle to the Overland Mail station at Ham Spring when Mr. Butterfield's stagecoach line began operations in 1858, till the war shut it down and the Yanks moved the line out of the South. Papa and our neighbor, Ben Earnhardt, also partnered up and contracted to deliver beef to the Army at Fort Belknap. When the Yankees left, Captain Earnhardt and Papa sold beef to the Texas militia and a Ranger company that took over the post. Grazing land was free. You just had to keep Indians, or neighbors, from stealing your cattle. I guess we made do, although I can remember Papa constantly saying: "We're cow poor."

To supplement his cattle income—whenever he actually got paid—Papa rode for the Rangers. So did Ben Earnhardt, who had been elected captain of the Jack County Rangers, Precinct 1. When I mention this to my friends here in Pennsylvania, they think Papa was some fast-shooting gunman chasing rustlers and outlaws all across Texas, but those kinds of Rangers didn't come about until well after the war. In the 1850s and 1860s, rangering companies pursued Indians. Papa drew $40 a month from the state—whenever Texas had enough money to pay him, that is.

Anyway, the state legislature carved out Jack County from some other counties in 1856, and a little settlement called Mesquiteville became the county seat. Within a year or two—I don't even know if old-timers in Jack County could tell you exactly when—Mesquiteville had been renamed Jacksboro.

Despite Indian raids, the loss of the Butterfield line, and a coming war, Jack County seemed to boom. Mama told me that maybe a thousand folks lived there by the time Texas went to war.

During those first weeks after Texas joined the Confederacy, war grew from mere rumor and braggadocio to something looming, real. . . .

From one end of the county to the other, folks held balls to honor our soldiers. Ladies stitched together uniforms, using crushed shells of walnuts and pecans to form a dye that turned the wool into a tan color. Butternut, not gray, but no one ever says: "My father wore the butternut." Or tan. Or brown. Or rags. It's always gray for the Rebels, and blue for the Yanks.

Papa only attended one of those shindigs, the one thrown by Gretchen Earnhardt, the captain's wife, since Papa and his partner would be riding to Harrisburg together, along with five other men that I did not know and would never get to know for they never returned.

Mama made me take a bath for the party. I wore pants, even brogans, and they dressed me up in a white shirt with a paper collar and a string tie that I thought might choke me to death. Felt like I was going to a funeral. I sure didn't like getting all duded up. I wasn't alone. Every kid and every grown-up had put on their best for Captain Earnhardt's ball.

In those days, children always accompanied their parents to dances, but we were left outside the barn to feast on ham and hominy, pies and cakes, potatoes and carrots. While our parents danced to the fiddlers and banjo men playing Stephen Foster and Irish melodies, we boys sat on the top rails of a round pen. The girls stayed by the table with all the food.

"I wish they'd let me go with 'em," Charley Conley said to me. Charley's father, Conn Conley, had been elected captain of the Jack County Seven, the name Mrs. Ida Mae McClure had given our brave Southern soldier boys. Everyone thought that Captain Earnhardt would merely transfer his rank from the Rangers to the Confederate Army, but Captain Earnhardt said he would rather fight than bark orders, and that his voice was raw enough from all the rangering he had been doing, that it was time to let somebody else command. Conn Conley wanted that job, and he got it. Not that it would hold, of course. Once they reached Harrisburg, even before they boarded the train bound for Virginia, Captain Conn Conley had been reduced in rank to Private Conn Conley and was taking orders from an Irish sergeant named Keegan. "Ain't fair," Charley said.

"No," I said, "it ain't fair." Mama would have tanned my hide had she heard me use the word *ain't*.

"I'd like to kill me a Yank."

"Me, too," I said, gnawing on a chicken leg.

Charley turned toward me. "What do you know about it? You ain't nothin' but a kid. And a runt, at that. You couldn't lift a musket, and you ain't even got no big front teeth yet to bite open the ca'tridge and pour powder down the barrel."

"My front teeth's comin' in!"

"Ain't."

"Is."

"Ain't."

"Is."

"Besides . . ." Charley tapped his thick finger against my chest. "You're ycllow to boot."

Well, all the boys, even the older ones approaching their teens, stared. Over at the table,

19

the girls looked our way, too, waiting for the commotion they sensed would soon erupt.

So I slammed the chicken leg bone in Charley's ear, knocking him off his perch, and dived on top of him.

Cheers and pain. Screams and grunts. That's what I remember, or what I think I remember about my first fight, based on what friends recalled over the next several years when the subject was brought up. I know I couldn't hear the music any more, as the half-broke horses in Ben Earnhardt's round pen began kicking up dust, stomping, and snorting, as if they were cheering us on.

Of course I lost. Charley was nine years old, already forking hay and chopping wood, and constantly getting whipped by the schoolmaster, Lasater, for fighting, so Charley had me out-muscled and outfoxed. He got on top of me, his big left hand on my throat, ignoring my feeble punches, with his right fist raised, ready to smash my nose. Just like that, he flew off me. I climbed to my feet, trying to see through the blinding dust and the beginning of tears. The girls and boys stopped cheering, but the horses kept dancing and whinnying. I steadied myself, trying to figure out where Charley was, when a hand grabbed my arm, and yanked me up off the ground.

"What's gotten into you two boys? You ain't disruptin' this ball. No, sir, you most certainly ain't. Your fathers goin' off to fight, and you two idgits is engagin' in fisticuffs."

As the dust settled, I was lowered back on the ground. By then, I could see Charley Conley as he came to his feet, and I felt some satisfaction that his nose was bleeding—even if I had not delivered that blow.

"You ain't touchin' me never again, you darky!" Charley yelled.

Down he went again. This time, he rolled over, tears flowing down his cheeks, but he did not try to stand and challenge the man who had broken up our fight.

I took a step away from the referee, and whispered: "Uncle Moses . . ."

"Shut up," Moses Gage hissed, and turned, his black face knotted and angry. "Charley . . . I'd expect such antics from him. But you, Pierce? You shame me. You shame your parents. You shame everyone. Ought to know better."

By now tears were carving ditches through the dirt caking my face. My head dropped. I shuffled my feet, staring at my dirty britches, my filthy shirt. My tie had been jerked open, and the paper collar was askew. Papa would whip me, most likely.

Obviously Moses Gage was not my uncle, but 'most everyone called him uncle. He was a man of color, but a freedman now, having been given his papers by his master over in Jefferson in 1851.

Since then, he had hunted in the Palo Pinto country, scouted for the Army and Rangers, traded with Indians, and traveled as far as the Llano Estacado and into the Indian Territory, and probably down into Mexico. For the past two years, he had worked, off and on, for Captain Earnhardt and Papa.

"I'll tell . . . ," Charley threatened.

"Tell what? That you was fightin' a mere child."

That got my hackles up, but I knew better than to open my mouth, having witnessed what Uncle Moses had done to Charley Conley.

"I'll tell that you . . ."

Moses Gage took another step toward Charley, who drew up his knees and flinched. "You tell that I pulled you off Master Pierce here. You tell that I tossed you on the ground. Go ahead, I'll wait for you." He backed up toward me, put his hands on his hips, and waited. "Go ahead. I'm waitin'."

Well, everyone in northwestern Texas knew about Moses Gage. They knew the story that when a band of Comanches had raided the Conley spread and ridden off with Charley's older sister, leaving their mother dead, it was Moses Gage who had ridden into Indian Territory, trading six horses and a Paterson Colt revolver for Janet Conley. Moses Gage had brought Charley's sister home.

Black man or not, he could have broken Charley's nose, and Conn Conley would have

22

likely thanked him, and offered him a snort of corn liquor and a cigar.

"Pierce," Uncle Moses said, "go help Charley up."

Naturally I obeyed.

"That's good. You two shake hands. Good. Now go wash the dirt off you. Hold your head back, Charley, that bleedin' will stop in a jiffy. You best look presentable when folks come out to take you-all home."

Moses Gage looked me in the eye. I always picture Uncle Moses as part Davy Crocket, part Pecos Bill, part Sam Houston, part Ulysses, and part Hercules. Only black. Close-cropped, salt-and-pepper hair, a slouch hat that matched his battered, scarred face, arms and legs as solid as cottonwoods, homespun shirt, buckskin britches, and store-bought boots. He let Charley's friends steer him to the water trough, but Uncle Moses led me to the porch of the Earnhardt cabin.

After filling a basin on a table with water from a porcelain pitcher, Uncle Moses dabbed his handkerchief into the water, wiping away my tears, the dirt, shaking his head.

"What are you doin' fightin' with trash like that, Pierce?" he asked.

"He tormented me," I said.

"That boy could stomp you to death. Sure is mean enough." He fixed my collar, and retied my tie.

For a boy my size and age, I thought I had done pretty fair.

"You'll be startin' school soon, Pierce," he said. "You look out for Charley Conley. He's the type that carries a grudge."

"Yes, sir."

He brushed off my trousers, and then stood up, tousling my hair, waiting for me to look at him, which, finally, I did.

Moses Gage smiled. "I think you'd've taken him," he said, "even little as you are."

I knew Uncle Moses was lying, but it still made me feel better. If my memory's right, I even smiled.

If Mama and Papa learned of the fight, brief as it was, neither said anything about it.

The next morning, back at our cabin, Papa saddled his dun mare, gathered up one gunny sack of food and another of extra socks, a spare shirt, and other sundries. Having no saddle scabbard, he sheathed his rifle in the long, fringed, blue woolen sock, and leaned his Enfield, which he had won off Captain Earnhardt back in '59 on a bet, against the hitching rail. Whenever Captain Earnhardt came by asking for Papa to ride with him after Indians, he would jest that Papa should bring "that ol' Enfield you stole from me."

Now Papa kissed Mama, and kneeled beside me, putting both hands on my shoulders.

"You'll take care of Mama, right?"

"Yes, sir."

Looking up at Mama, he said: "Moses'll be by every now and then." He wet his lips. "Austin isn't that far away, you know."

Mama's voice came out soft but strong, certain. "This is our home, Wil."

He cleared his throat. "It'll be our home when this ruction is over, too. Don't forget that."

She did not respond, and Papa looked back at me, smiling. Even back then, a smile from him was rare.

"Be a good boy," he said, and pulled me close, hugging me tightly, which felt strange, Papa never being one to show much emotion. This embrace lasted for what felt like an eternity, before he pushed himself to his feet, knees popping. Then he grabbed the Enfield, and swung into the saddle.

"Best be getting along," he said. "Reckon everyone's already gathered at the Conley place."

Still, Mama did not speak.

"I'll write," he said, and neck-reined the dun.

"Yes." Mama had found her voice, but now it cracked. "Do that."

We watched Papa ride off toward the creek, which he would follow to town, the Conleys being townsfolk since Mrs. Conley had been called to Glory and Janet having refused to live far from people after her abduction by Indians.

Even after Papa was long out of view, Mama stood there, watching the dust settle, watching the emptiness. That night, I heard her cry, which I had not heard her do before, not realizing just how many of these men would not be coming home.

CHAPTER TWO

At first, the only difference that I could see was that Papa wasn't there. That, of course, made a big difference. Mama busied herself, working sunup to sundown, milking the cow, gathering the eggs, chopping firewood, and teaching me my letters and numbers. The letters—the reading—I took to heartily. The numbers, the cyphering . . . well . . . that would never be my strongest talent.

Captain Earnhardt's oldest boy, Clarke, came by about every third day to check on us. Clarke was sixteen years old, a wiry kid with broad shoulders who rode as if he were born in a saddle. He looked nothing like the captain. Folks said he took after his mother, but I never agreed with that assessment—because I never once saw Gretchen Earnhardt with a chaw of tobacco bulging out of her cheek. Seldom did I see Clarke Earnhardt without chewing tobacco.

"I could trail Clarke Earnhardt real easy," I remember telling Uncle Moses when he was trying to show me how to track a deer. "Just follow the brown stains he leaves every thirty or forty rods."

Never had I heard Uncle Moses laugh so hard.

When the preacher came by to hold service every third Sunday, it began to strike me just how Jack County had changed. The Jack County Seven were not the only ones who had joined the Cause. Now, a lot of the men in that area were not what you would call regular church-goers. Sunday was just another day to them, even to Papa. The only men we would see at the meeting hall were old-timers, or the young ones who attended Mr. Lasater's school. Our choir had no bass singers.

Most of the men, and some boys, had joined regiments that went up to Missouri and Arkansas. A few remained down on the Texas coast. Some even returned to their home states to serve in units from Kentucky, Tennessee, Louisiana. More than a few who wore the blue didn't come back to Texas after the war. They had nothing to come home to. Branded Unionists, their homes were burned, their livestock confiscated, and their families driven out of the state.

By the fall, we had heard from Papa. He had joined the 1st Texas Infantry, which consisted of mostly East Texas and South Texas men, like Uncle Jake. A colonel named Wigfall commanded them. I had thought that Captain Earnhardt would have been put in charge for sure. They were in the Potomac District of Virginia. I didn't know where Virginia was. Mama had to draw a map in the dirt, pointing out where she had been born in Greensboro, North Carolina, and next showing me the state just above that, which she said was Virginia. The Potomac was a river, and right above that lay Yankee country.

"Then they're right close to the Yankees," I said.

She bit her lip, nodded, and hurried back into the barn to find some eggs.

That close to Yankees. The thought excited me, because I knew Papa would soon be fighting in a real war. He would come back with stories of glory and blood and thunder, which certainly seemed a whole lot more exciting that the drudgery of living on a hardscrabble Jack County ranch.

Of course, in Papa's first letter, which Mama read every night, sometimes more than once, all Uncle Jake and Captain Earnhardt and Papa seemed to be doing was marching or drilling or following orders barked by that Irish sergeant from Nacogdoches. They didn't like him. They didn't like orders. They certainly didn't like all that walking. They didn't like Virginia and its ticks and mosquitoes, nor its swamps and hills, and when the cold killed off the mosquitoes and ticks, they didn't like the frost and how bone-numbing the cold could make a body feel in that country.

Back home, things got cold, too. The first blue

norther hit in late September, ending summer in a matter of hours and coating everything with sleet and freezing rain.

In December of 1861, the state legislature passed an act that allowed for the raising of another Rangering company, to replace the boys we had lost to the Confederate Army. Jack, Young, Palo Pinto, and Parker countics formed one company. Clarke Earnhardt joined that one. The various companies were stationed from the Red River to the Río Grande. Clarke Earnhardt and twenty or twenty-five other men went to Fort Belknap.

"Are the Yankees gonna invade us, too?" I asked Mama.

She forced that smile, and tousled my hair. "Pierce, you don't have to worry about Yankees. 'And ye shall hear of wars and rumors of wars: see that ye be not troubled: for all these things must come to pass, but the end is not yet.'" She gave me that inquiring stare I had seen far too often.

"John," I guessed.

"Matthew," she corrected. "I see we should read the Bible more."

No, it wasn't Yankees that the settlers along the northern Texas frontier feared. The Rangers—sometimes known as Minute Men—had been organized as a defense against the Comanches and Kiowas.

All these years later, I think about things I remember, but somehow never noticed back in those days.

The butt of that pocket revolver, a .32-caliber Whitney, protruding from Mama's apron. A Mississippi rifle leaning against the wall by the door . . . or right next to Mama's bed . . . or by the well, the barn, the corral, the woodpile . . . never far from her reach. So many things we did back then I looked at as adventures, as when Uncle Moses would ride by and suggest that it was a good day for Mama and me to go to Jacksboro, mentioning that we could see what candy Mr. Goldman might have at his mercantile. Then, once in town, Mama would decide it was too late to return home, so we would spend the night at some friend's home. Sometimes, we might stay two days.

Other times, Uncle Moses would accompany us on a ride over to visit Gretchen Earnhardt and her family, and we'd stay there for two days or more. Once, we even rode all the way to Fort Belknap, ostensibly to pay a visit to Clarke Earnhardt. What struck me that time was just how many people from nearby ranches had decided to come to the fort. Many of them didn't even know Clarke Earnhardt.

"What happened to our chickens, Mama?" I remember asking once when Uncle Moses and six other riders escorted us back to the ranch after a few days away.

"Coyot's must have gotten them, Pierce. . . . Don't fret, son. We'll get some more real soon, and coyot's got to eat, too."

We didn't get any more chickens until long after the war.

In the spring of '62, Mama decided that it was time I started school. I wanted to rebel, but knew better. Besides, Mama said I could practice my reading on Papa's letters home.

Passages from some of those are etched in my brain, too.

March 1862: *Oh how we wish this war would close.*

June 1862: *Bacon costs $1.25 a pound, but the sutlers do not charge anything extra for the mold, rot, and worms. Nor do the sutlers remove their thumbs surreptitiously placed on the scales.*

August 1862: *Your letter arrived yesterday, wrapped in a pair of socks. I cannot thank you enough for both. The letter warmed my heart. The socks soothed my feet after another long march.*

For a man who rarely spoke, Papa showed himself to be a man of letters—to my way of thinking now, even though I hardly noticed back then.

One letter came in late October, but Mama never let me read that one. Most letters she would read over and over, till the ink faded or the paper crumbled, but this one she read once, silently, tears running down her cheeks, then she stuck it back into its envelope and into the pocket of her apron.

"Mama?" I called to her.

She did not seem to hear.

"Is Papa . . . ?" My own choking voice brought her out of whatever thoughts Papa's letter had sent her into, and she looked at me, wiping her face, smiling the saddest smile I had ever seen.

"Your father is fine, Pierce. So is Jacob. As well as can be expected. Bedtime."

I do not know what became of that letter. It wasn't until years later that I thought I knew what had been in that letter.

Ah, but school. I had dreaded it, but soon grew to love it. Mr. Lasater was an excellent teacher, and I especially enjoyed the whippings he gave Charley Conley. I never felt his paddle or ruler. He showed patience with me, even giving me personal attention when it came to math. Why he liked me was simple. I was an attentive student, and, at six years old, I read, and read well—thanks to my mother. That prompted a few fights at recess with Charley Conley, and Mr. Lasater always came to my rescue.

What I did not like was how I got to school. School was six miles from our place, along a trail and even a road. Mama walked me there sometimes. Other times we would ride double on one of our horses. Now, as a boy, the last thing you want your friends and enemies at school to see is your mother bringing you there. Which led to more fights, including one—probably in the autumn of '63—that got me in trouble with Mr. Lasater.

"Pierce Braden, you do not strike a girl. Never!"

"She said I'm a baby. Called me a girl."

"That is no reason to hit a girl."

"She's no girl. She's Nancy Livermore."

"You will apologize to her, young man. You will never strike her, or any of the fairer sex, again. If you do, by thunder, you will do arithmetic problems from the time you are in your seat to the time I tell you that it is time for you to leave for home."

A hard thing to do, apologizing to Nancy Livermore. Especially since I had to do it in front of the entire class, with Charley Conley sitting in the corner with his dunce cap on, giggling and pointing his finger at me. And Mr. Lasater doing nothing to make him stop.

Nancy was a slender girl, two years my senior, with long brown hair in pigtails, and hazel eyes. She was standing at the head of the class, right in front of Mr. Lasater's desk. I walked up to her, head down and shuffling my feet.

"Sorry," I said.

From the doorway, Mr. Lasater called out: "Look at her, Master Braden!"

So I looked up. Had to, or face addition and subtraction forever. That's when I felt really bad because I could see the redness where my fingers had slapped her cheek. I could see how she had been crying, the pained look on her face mixed with the embarrassment I had caused the both of us as we stood before eighteen students— and Charley Conley, who I would never call a "student."

"I'm sorry, Nancy!" I wailed. "I won't ever hit you again."

Which, of course, caused Charley Conley to laugh even louder.

Thankfully that angered Mr. Lasater enough to haul Charley off the stool, knock off his dunce cap, and lead him outside to the well for another whipping.

Mama stopped escorting me to school after that, but still I wouldn't walk. She wouldn't let me go those six miles alone. She refused to let me ride, either, so it became Uncle Moses's chore. To see that I got to school all right, and home.

No one said anything about Uncle Moses serving as my protector. No one called me a girl or a sissy. Not even Charley Conley said anything. They all remembered what had happened at the Earnhardt place when Charley and I first brawled.

Yup, Moses Gage put the fear of the wrath of the Lord into all of those kids, much more than Mr. Lasater's paddle.

When winter came, though, things changed. Mama would bundle me up, and let me walk to school. She said I knew my way by then, and Moses Gage had plenty of work to keep him busy. Come spring, however, she appeared to have forgotten that I knew my way. Uncle Moses, or sometimes another hired hand from Captain Earnhardt's spread, came to escort me to school.

I preferred going to school with the captain's hired men. They rode horseback, told me stories I would never dare repeat in front of Mama or Mrs. Earnhardt or even Nancy Livermore. Sometimes, when we were a hundred yards or so from the school, the hired men would stop, dismount, and let me ride to school alone, leaving Charley Conley and all the other kids amazed, speechless. Even more impressive was that I somehow got out of the saddle and onto the ground without tasting gravel. I would wrap the reins around the post, grab my lunch pail and flour sack filled with books, and walk to the playground, trying to match the bowlegged strides of those old cowhands.

Of course, after Mr. Lasater would ring the bell, and we would go inside for our studies, my horse would wander off. Or so most of my classmates thought.

There's another bit of conversation, I recall, that must have happened in the spring of '64.

Nancy Livermore was waiting for me after school. We'd volunteered to help Mr. Lasater with some cleaning. She swept the floors, and I cleaned the slates. She finished first, but was sitting on the steps when I walked out, covered in chalk and dirt.

"How many horses do you own, Pierce?"

I almost answered: "Three." But stopped and shrugged. "What do you care?"

She opened a notebook. "Because this week you rode up on a blood bay on Thursday, a zebra dun on Friday. You must have walked the other days. Two weeks ago, you came on two blacks. One had two white stockings. The other had a blaze. Last month, I counted twelve other horses. Not counting the times you walked or Moses Gage brought you to school."

"Lots of people in Texas have lots of horses," I let her know.

"But most of them know how to tether or hobble their horses. All of yours wander off."

She knew. She beamed. My face reddened with embarrassment.

"Don't worry," she said. "I won't tell."

"Tell what?"

Nancy Livermore gave me the look, and I quickly confessed. "All right. Those horses belong to the men who ride for Captain Earnhardt."

"I know that. I've seen Hog Clagett at Pa's saloon in Jacksboro. He favors the black with the two stocking feet, but I've also seen him ride that high-prancing blue roan and some of those brown ponies you've come in on. Ellis Morrell, he favors that zebra dun, and he wears those spurs

36

with the big Mexican rowels. Which explains how come that horse is so skittish, and those scars on its sides. I've never seen you with a pair of spurs, Pierce Braden. And Yorker Nott? He drinks too much John Barleycorn. So I've seen his blood bay at the hitching rail in front of Pa's saloon more times than I've seen Charley Conley get a whupping. But I still won't tell."

"How come?"

"Because I like you." She batted her eyes, and offered me her hand so that I could help her to her feet. Seeing how she had me dead to rights and could ruin the respect I'd gotten from several classmates, I immediately pulled her up.

She stood inches from me, towering over me because all of the Livermores stood lean, sturdy, and tall.

Next thing I knew, Nancy Livermore had leaned over and kissed me full on the lips.

As I told Mama that night: "I fell over and stars flew out of my head."

But the war would end our budding romance. The following week, with the grass greening up and the moon full, I found myself taking another visit to Fort Belknap. The Earnhardts were there, as well as other ranchers, but the Livermores and the Conleys were townsfolk, so they didn't leave the safety of Jacksboro, and since the bulk of the people who paid Mr. Lasater's salary lived in town, he taught school there, too.

We stayed a week. When Uncle Moses rode in with the Rangers, he eased his spotted horse up to where Mama stood doing laundry with a group of other women. Clarke Earnhardt rode up alongside him, grinning grimly at his mother.

"Missus Braden." Moses tipped his hat.

"Moses." Mama's lips remained tight.

"How's your mama and daddy doing down in Austin?" he asked her.

She nodded, but it took her a long time to answer. "I'm planning on going to see them this week." Her voice sounded forced, and she wiped her face with the soaking, soapy shirt she held.

I sprang to my feet. I had been helping the women with their chores, although I'd overheard some old-timer say: "Boy dirties up the clothes. Women do it ag'in. Don't say nothin' to that runt. Reckon it keeps 'em busy, keeps their minds off things, so they don't mind."

"We're going to see Grandpa?" I piped in.

"Yes, Pierce," Mama said, still looking at Uncle Moses, whose head bobbed slightly.

"Mighty good idea, ma'am. You tell your folks that Uncle Moses Gage tells 'em 'howdy.'"

"And Mister Blackburn asked if you'd pay him a visit, Ma," Clarke Earnhardt said to his mother.

"It would be good to see Omar," Mrs. Earnhardt said. Her voice came across as about as stiff and forced as Mama's.

I tossed the shirt into the soapy water, shook my

head, and asked Mama if I could go to the privy. She didn't answer, even after I asked a second time, so I just nodded at Uncle Moses and walked to the latrines the Rangers had dug. Ask me, they'd dug way too many for a company of twenty-five men.

Folks treated me like a kid, like I was some fool, and it sickened me, angered me. I stormed off toward the latrine, not caring about the smell, the flies. Hearing a horse's *clopping* behind me, I stopped before I made my way up that hill.

"That stinks, don't it?" Uncle Moses said.

Sighing, I turned around. He was mounted on his horse, one leg crooked over the horn, reins draped over the horse's neck, tamping his pipe for a smoke.

"It stinks," I said, and he got my meaning.

"How old are you, Master Pierce?"

"Turned ten in April," I let him know.

The pipe lowered. He glared.

I corrected myself. "I turned eight in April."

"And you know everything, I reckon."

"I know enough."

"Like what?"

"That we ain't going home, that we're going to see Grandma and Grandpa in Austin, but it ain't because Mama wants to do no visiting."

"Don't say *ain't,* Master Pierce." Moses lit his pipe, shook out the match, and tossed it to the ground. "Your schoolteacher won't like to hear it, especially comin' out of your mouth. Your ma'll be angered."

"You say it," I snapped back.

"Ain't as smart as you."

I walked up to him. His horse lifted its head, and I stopped.

"I'm smart enough to know why we're going to Austin. It's Indians."

He nodded. "I figgered as much. You've always been a bright one, Master Pierce."

"Same reason Mama never lets me go to school on my own. Other kids do." I knew, of course, other kids lived closer to school, or walked with neighbors, and a few of the older boys came to school with rifles or shotguns, even a revolver or two.

"You go by yourself sometimes," Uncle Moses reminded me.

I nodded. "Yeah. In winter. Before school lets out. When everybody knows the Comanches and Kiowas are huddled up in their villages." I pointed at the grass. "It's spring. Moon's full. I lived here long enough to know it's a raiding moon. You don't have to treat me like I don't know nothing."

"You'll enjoy Austin," he said. "Good to see your grandfolks. Wish I could visit mine, but I don't know where to look for 'em, or if any of 'em's even alive."

"Well," I said, "I'd rather go back to my home.

Our home." My head bobbed with the finality of my argument.

Uncle Moses drew on his pipe stem, looked back at the women huddled together by the baskets of laundry and tubs of water. Smoke rose toward his battered hat as he looked back at me.

"Son," he said, "you ain't got no home to go back to."

CHAPTER THREE

Living in Austin turned out to be an adjustment. With no threat of Indians, I could walk to school—which happened to be just four blocks from the home of Grandpa Adair and Grandma Beatrice. At Miss Madelyn's school, I learned how smart most eight- and nine-year-olds were. Back home in Jack County, Mr. Lasater had lauded my skills. In Travis County, Miss Madelyn Cox corrected my English and saddled me with arithmetic and geology and science and more multiplication and division and addition and subtraction. Then, as punishment, she gave me extra arithmetic.

More than once I felt the urge to sneak out of Austin and steal my way back to Jacksboro. Then came the sad news. Mr. Lasater had left for Alabama. Jacksboro had been forced to close the school.

Here today in Pennsylvania, when we talk about the war, most of my fellow miners and engineers say how blessed I was to have grown up in Texas, so far removed from the "real" war. Nothing significant happened in Texas, not when you think about the carnage witnessed at places such as Gettysburg and Atlanta, Vicksburg and Manassas, Shiloh and, of course, Sharpsburg, the last a battle that I would learn much about in the years to come, a battle I would imagine myself fighting, only this time, I would lead Hood's 1st Texas to victory.

Memoirs of generals and the histories of that awful war rarely mention the Texas home front. Yes, we were far removed, in more ways than one.

"Don't believe a thing you read in the *State Gazette*," Grandpa Adair told us as Mama had me reading the newspaper. "Last summer, those fools printed that General Lee was whipping the Yankees, had captured the capital of Pennsylvania, and even Washington City. Then we learned what had really happened at Gettysburg."

Austin was the capital of Texas, and more than twenty-five hundred whites and more than one thousand slaves—plus a dozen or so freedmen—called the city home. It boasted the Capitol, the governor's mansion, and other buildings. Sometimes, we would take Sunday afternoon drives to look at the mansions being built. Yet it was also a city without a railroad, without a telegraph pole, without much industry—although the war had changed that somewhat by the time Mama and I knocked on the door of my grandparents' home.

In some ways, Austin resembled Jacksboro. Rugged, coarse, a regular frontier village. Only Austin was much greener. It was hilly, covered with cedar and hardwood trees, and, surrounded by the Colorado River, Waller Creek, and Shoal Creek, it definitely had more water.

"Bath, Pierce," Mama often ordered.

"But . . . Mama . . . I took one last week."

"Bath."

War news was as scarce in Austin as it was in Jack County. In fact, by the time we arrived in May of '64, everything had become scarce.

Pins, needles, shoes, even salt—things were hard to come by, thanks to the Yankee blockade. Forget about coffee. Grandma Beatrice took to burning acorns and manufacturing something that Mama and Grandpa Adair could call coffee. I walked to school in my bare feet, as did many kids, and in patched clothes because most clothing was being shipped to our soldiers far from Texas. Newspapers became thinner due to the shortage of paper.

The lack of paper made it harder for Mama to write letters to Papa. She took to ripping out the front pages of books, or using the back of peeling wallpaper, then she would fold those into envelopes, and head over to the postmaster's, where she would hope to receive a letter from Papa. By the fall of 1864, however, we rarely heard from Papa.

On those nights, I lay in the trundle bed and tried to pretend that I was not hearing my mother cry herself to sleep. It had become a common occurrence.

Like Jack County, Travis County had voted against Secession, and like Jack County men, Travis County men backed the Southern cause once war broke out. Grandpa Adair served on the Texas State Military Board, which established a textile mill in the state penitentiary in Huntsville as well as war factories in Austin—one that made percussion caps, and a foundry that produced cannon. Yet Grandpa's main job, to me, appeared to be criticizing the governor, the legislature, the generals, the war effort.

"The Lone Star refused to let a room to Senator Garrison," I remember him saying. "Bully for that innkeeper. Garrison wound up in Sol's wagon yard, and he had to use his diamond stickpin to pay."

By that time, a dollar was worth two-and-a-half cents. By that time, tobacco and nails became tools of bartering. Once, on our Sunday afternoon drive, Grandpa drove Mama and me to the Capitol, where he pointed at the tents and wagons parked along the grounds.

"That's where our representatives are staying for the session," he said. "Because they can't get a room in town. If they'd leave it up to me, I'd run the whole sorry lot down to Mexico."

We ate cornbread and pork, pork and cornbread, and, sometimes, just cornbread.

So, no, we were not that far away from that "real" war.

We felt it—rather, Grandpa Adair felt it—in property and poll taxes and taxes on just about everything, from services to distilling to income. We felt it, too, in other ways. Bandits ruled the highways in the Hill Country to the west.

And up north, back home in Jack County?

Letters from Papa might have stopped, but sometime during the winter of 1864, Mama got one from Gretchen Earnhardt. I have it yet, handed down from Mama, and though it remains hard to read, I include it below:

30 Oct. '64
Jack County, Tex.
My dearest friend Martha:

I take pencil in hand in hoping that all is well with you and Pierce, who I imagine has grown even taller than he was when you departed this past spring.

By now news has likely reached you of the terrible calamity that fell among our neighbors in Young County on the 13th of this month, but rest assured that Clarke and I remain unharmed.

45

Mildred Durkin is dead. So is the Negro Britt Johnson's son. Both butchered and scalped by the red heathens who struck Elm Creek with such barbarity. Mildred's mother, Mrs. FitzGerald, was taken captive by the red devils. So were Mildred's daughters, and some Negroes.

You know of the Frontier Organization, I am sure, or what Clarke calls "our flop-eared militia"—those cowards who, unlike our brave husbands, have come to the frontier to defend us rather than be conscripted into the Confederate Army. Today, I suppose that many of them wish they were with General Hood, glory to his name and those brave Texans who serve with him.

A company of soldiers rode after the fiendish Kiowas and Comanches, but were outsmarted by the cunning savages. Five soldiers are dead.

They struck us, too, in the early morning. I do not know if these were the same Indians who had attacked our friends on Elm Creek, but they were well-armed. Poor Yorker Nott is dead. I don't think he ever knew what killed him, and I will not sicken you with details of what those heathens did to him after his death. Trying to save the horses in our round pen, Hog

Clagett suffered grievous wounds, and would likely have been called to Glor had not Ellis Morrell and Uncle Moses charged off the devils. The Indians managed to scalp Hog, but he rests now in Ben's bed, and is mending. He says when he is able to ride again, he will cross the Red River and kill the first Indian he sees, and pin that scalp on his head to replace the hair that Comanche took from him. Knowing Hog, he means it.

Uncle Moses and Ellis are unscathed.

The barbarians killed all of our dogs, though, and took off ten horses. We have not quite figured out how many cattle are gone.

But, blessed be the Lord, my children are safe. I cannot imagine what Mrs. FitzGerald is going through, and find some comfort in that poor Mildred is no longer suffering.

Oh, would to God that this war is over, and that your Wil and my Ben were home now.

You were smart to leave this country when you did, Martha. I hope someone will be here to greet you when, God willing, you and Pierce and Wil return home.

Yours truly,
Gretchen Earnhardt

No war in Texas? I must differ. There was a war going on in that state, just against a different enemy.

Twelve men and women died in what became known as the Elm Creek Raid. Seven women and children were kidnapped; most of those would be ransomed—many by another Negro, Britt Johnson—and returned home by the end of the following year.

The next letter Mama received from Gretchen Earnhardt came from Fort Belknap, where she had moved her family, permanently, until the war's end. Ellis Morrell would form yet another company of militia, and he, Uncle Moses, and other settlers would patrol that part of Jack County against marauding Indians.

There's another story that comes to mind, but I cannot say if it is true. If Gretchen Earnhardt ever wrote Mama about it, my mother didn't keep the letter, or ever let me read it.

By the spring of 1865, Ben Earnhardt returned home to Jack County. He took over the militia Ellis Morrell had formed. He took Mrs. Earnhardt and Clarke back to the ranch. No one ever spoke of this—certainly not to Ben Earnhardt's face—but he had not been reassigned, nor had he been transferred from Hood's Texas Brigade to the Lost Creek Minute Men. He had deserted.

His wife had written him, telling him about the Elm Creek Raid, the scalping of Hog Clagett, the death of Yorker Nott. That proved too much for a fighting man, a Texan, like Ben Earnhardt. By late December 1864, he—and practically all that was left of the 1st Texas—knew the fate of the Army of Northern Virginia, of the Confederate States of America. There was no reason to stick it out, fight for this forlorn hope. So he quit, took the ankle express out of Virginia, dodging both Confederate provosts and Yankee patrols. By February, he had made it home to Jack County.

No one came looking for him—and Captain Earnhardt was not alone. The Confederate Army lost scores of Texans to desertion. Fighting for the "Lost Cause" was one thing, but the threat of Indians destroying their homes and their families brought many back from the battlefields and camps in Virginia and Tennessee.

But not Papa.

Mama did get one letter from Captain Earnhardt, just a short note he mailed after his homecoming. Mama cherished that one, cried, showed it to Grandma, to Grandpa, to me, and cried some more.

Dear martha, the letter began.

> am home in Jack co. wil & jake wer in fine Spirits & Health when I left dont worry about them They ar to tuf to get kilt
> > your nehbor
> > B.P. Earnhardt

Word came through the newspapers of the slaughter at Franklin, Tennessee, the fall of Atlanta, loss after loss in Virginia. The preacher at Grandma's church told us that we should not fear, but persevere. Newspapers, the few still printing, reported that Governor Murrah was begging his fellow Texans not to quit, to keep up the fight, but, by that point in time, blue-coats were crossing Texas. Rip Ford, that gallant leader of Texas fighting men, whipped the Yankees all the way down in South Texas at Palmito Ranch.

That victory came on May 13, 1865.

That's when captured Yanks started telling Rip Ford's boys that Rebel Army after Rebel Army had started begging for a truce, waving the white flag, asking for peace. That's when we finally learned what had happened at Appomattox, Virginia, that Robert E. Lee had surrendered the Army of Northern Virginia.

That's when Mama and Grandma fell to their knees, and prayed, begged that God had spared Papa and Uncle Jake, that through all God's mercy, He would see that they got home. That's the only time I ever saw Grandpa Adair cry.

"You mean the war's over?" I asked.

Mama pulled me close, buried my head underneath her bosom. "Yes. Yes, Glory to God, the war is over."

"Maybe," Grandpa Adair said, sniffling. "But

just because Lee's called it quits, don't mean the rest of our boys will give up the fight."

But they did, even in Texas.

In early June, General Kirby Smith surrendered his army to Yankee General Edward Canby. As Grandpa Adair said: "Smith didn't even wait for the ink to dry. As soon as he put his mark on that paper . . . for I daresay Kirby Smith didn't have the brains to learn how to write his name . . . he took off for Mexico."

Well, General Smith had company. Governor Murrah decided to vacate Austin for the safer climes south of the border. Ed Clark, who had also served as Texas governor, fled, too. Missouri patriot Jo Shelby crossed the Río Grande. So did scores of other Confederates. Some merely wanted to fight some more. Most of them wanted to avoid a hangman's noose. Since President Abraham Lincoln had been assassinated, government officials and high-ranking officers thought they might be tried, convicted, and executed as war criminals. Most of these men, eventually, would come back. But not Governor Murrah. He was a lunger, and the consumption killed him in Monterrey shortly after he fled Texas.

My mother's and grandparents' joy—and my disappointment: *Papa lost the war! How could that be?*—did not last long.

That night, I remember being huddled in the root cellar with Mama, Grandma Beatrice, and even Grandpa Adair, with no candle, just ourselves. You could taste the fear. Austin had turned into bedlam. Men and women, even children—black and white—looted Austin warehouses. We could hear the gunshots sounding across the city. Our brave government officials had fled Austin in such a hurry, they left the state treasury unguarded. Former Confederate soldiers went inside and walked out with some $17,000.

Don't think that that money was worthless Confederate and state script. It was in gold and silver.

Two weeks later, a general named Granger landed in Galveston with a bunch of bluecoats. That was June 19th. Granger announced that every slave was now free, Confederate laws no longer could be enforced, that cotton was public property, and that the Union Army controlled the state of Texas.

On the 25th of July, bluecoats from the 18th New York Cavalry arrived in Austin. They brought with them a lawyer from Austin named Andrew Jackson Hamilton, escorting him into the state Capitol.

Earlier, I mentioned that Travis County had voted against Secession back in 1861. Well, according to Grandpa Adair, the biggest Yankee-loving cur was Andrew Jackson Hamilton. "He had to run for his life," Grandpa said. "Folks in town hated him so much . . . even those of us who stood against Secession . . . he wouldn't have been tarred and feathered, but drawn and quartered."

Hamilton had left in 1862, and had backed the blue.

Now he was back in Austin, the new governor of Texas. The *Federal* governor of Texas.

Reconstruction had begun. The war had been over for three months.

Yet Papa still had not come home.

CHAPTER FOUR

Webb Clayton was the first of my Austin classmates' fathers to return home.

Actually Webb Clayton came home before Wesley Merritt and his Yanks rode into Austin, or even before the Federals landed at Galveston, freed the slaves, and Yankee rule went into effect. Webb Clayton walked into his shack just a few weeks before everyone understood that, indeed, the war was over. That the South had lost.

Grandpa Adair didn't think much of Webb Clayton, as a Confederate soldier or as a man, and Grandma Beatrice thought even less of him.

"White trash," Grandma Beatrice said, spitting snuff into her tin can. "Nothing but trash. All the Claytons. They's all trash."

"Mother . . ." Mama tilted her head in my direction.

Grandma Beatrice glared. "Well, he is. All the Claytons. Trash. Nothing but trash."

She wiped her mouth, and snorted, and I began to wonder if that made Mary Jane Clayton trash, too. Mary Jane hardly said anything at school, never answered any of the questions the schoolteacher asked. I didn't mind Mary Jane so much, though I couldn't call us friends. I don't think she had a friend in school, but, well, she made me look smart.

Grandpa Adair joined the assault on that white trash Clayton family.

"He wasn't no soldier, by grab," Grandpa bellowed. "Never fired a shot. Went up to guard them bluebellies at Camp Ford, the craven wonder."

Located just outside of Tyler in a region that Texans called the Piney Woods—Papa would remark that East Texas might as well have been part of Louisiana—Camp Ford was a prison that swelled with captured Yankees after the Federals' disastrous Red River campaign late in the war. Prisons, I figured, had to have soldiers to keep an eye on all of those prisoners, but Grandpa sure had little use for prison guards.

"And you know what I heard?" Grandpa Adair nodded, as if whatever he had heard at the tavern was bona-fide gospel. "I heard that when word reached that prison camp about the surrender, they just unlocked the gates, walked home. Now,

54

what if that had just been rumor? Tell me that. Why, those thousands of Yanks would have been freed to arm themselves and march upon us down here in Austin. It could have turned the war, it could have. Could have . . ."

By then, Mama had grabbed my hand. She knew she was outnumbered, and that this was one battle she would never win. We went upstairs to read from the Bible, leaving Grandma spitting into her hand-held cuspidor and nodding in agreement with her husband.

As we walked up the stairs, I could still hear Grandma Beatrice. "White trash." *Spit.* "Nothing but trash." *Spit.*

After motioning me to sit on the bed, Mama grabbed the Bible off the table.

"Are the Claytons white trash?" I asked.

The Bible closed.

"That's not a phrase I'd care for you to repeat, Pierce."

"Grandma Beatrice says it."

"She says a lot of things."

That was true, and had I repeated some of Grandma Beatrice's words, Mama would have sent me to the woods to fetch a switch, which she would have then used on my backside.

The Bible opened.

"Mama?"

"Yes, Pierce?"

"What does 'white trash' mean?"

The Bible closed.

She held it on her lap, pursing her lips, trying to think how she should answer. "Mostly," she said after the longest while, "it means poor."

I remembered Papa. "Like 'cow poor'?" I asked.

Her face brightened with her smile, although her eyes soon glistened with tears.

"I suppose. Something like that anyway."

"So . . . we're poor."

This time she actually laughed. "Most definitely, Pierce. We are most definitely poor."

"White trash?"

Her head shook. "That I would not say. And we are poor in money, Son, but not in spirit. Not in health. Certainly, not in love. And the Claytons, they are poor, too. Very poor. Not cow poor . . . they just . . . struggle. Life for them is hard, much more than it is for our family, so you count your blessings, Son. But I would not consider them white trash, no matter what Mama and Papa call them."

My head bobbed, though I did not understand anything she had said, except that we were poor, but not white trash.

The Bible opened, and Mama read.

Burt Pirkle was the next soldier we knew to return to Austin. Pirkle's son, Bobby Ray, also attended our school, and lived only ten doors down from Grandma and Grandpa's place. Bobby Ray was three years my senior, but we were friends. Anyway, we had been friends, until his father came home from the war.

He practically beat down our front door one Saturday morning, causing Grandma Beatrice to mutter and complain and secretly curse as Grandpa Adair let the tow-headed kid race into our parlor.

"I gotta see Pierce, sir!" Bobby Ray bellowed.

Down the stairs I flew, hearing Grandma Beatrice scream: "Watch that sword, Bobby Ray Pirkle! You knife my sofa, and I'll whup you to a frazzle, boy!"

"Ain't no sword, Missus Pierce!" Bobby Ray hollered.

Spying me, he waved a bayonet high over his head, almost knocking over a candlestick, causing both of my grandparents to cringe. He also cut loose with a high-pitched yell as Grandpa Adair chased both Bobby Ray Pirkle and me out the front door.

There had been no school since news of the surrender. We children did not mind. Perhaps we had lost the war, but, to us children, having no school felt like the greatest victory in the world. Maybe no one knew what to teach, now that we were under Federal law. I thought our Readers would need to be replaced by books by Lincoln or Grant or somebody like that.

Now here stood Bobby Ray Pirkle, and he had brought the war to me.

I stared in awe at the bayonet.

"Pa brung it home," Bobby Ray told me. We sat on the verandah. I started to touch it, but he jerked it back. "Taken it off a dead Yank, Pa done," Bobby Ray said. "He tol' me. Kilt that Yank at Perryville. Yes, sir, Pa kilt that Yank deader'n a doorknob. Kilt him deader'n dirt. I bet Pa kilt a thousand Yanks. He was a horse soldier, you know. Colonel Harrison made him a capt'n, you know."

He held the bayonet, thrust it like he was a musketeer. Finally he let me touch it. But only briefly.

Around the same time my father was enlisting in Hood's Texas Brigade, Burt Pirkle had joined the 8th Texas Cavalry. He had brought along a Navy Colt, a Bowie knife, a saddle, bridle, and blanket. Benjamin Franklin Terry, the commanding officer, had made Burt Pirkle go to the nearest store and buy a carbine. His army would provide the horse.

They became known as Terry's Texas Rangers, probably the second-most famous Confederate unit to fight out the war. Behind, I must proudly brag, Hood's boys.

Terry was at some battle in Kentucky—the name, and much more of the regimental history I would learn from a ranch hand back home—but his regiment, subsequently commanded by colonels named Lubbock (briefly) and Thomas Harrison (for the war's duration), would serve with distinction in battles at Shiloh—Pittsburg Landing, as the Yankees called it; Murfreesboro— Stones River, as the Yankees called it; Chickamauga and Chattanooga, where both North and South apparently agreed on the name; as well as other campaigns. They had fought at Bentonville, North Carolina, in one of the last major battles of the war.

Bobby Ray Pirkle told me: "Gen'ral Johnston surrendered at Durham Station, but Pa an' a lot of us other Rangers"—it seemed that Bobby Ray now thought that because he had been given a bayonet, he had served with Terry's Texas Rangers, too—"well, we decided to keep the fight a-goin'."

After slipping through the Northern lines, the Rangers began making their way east, hoping to join up with some Confederates who had not surrendered. By the time they had reached Alabama, they knew the hopelessness of the Cause. After splitting up, they rode home.

I don't know if Burt Pirkle ever took the oath of allegiance to the Union. Like many former Confederates—I imagine that Ben Earnhardt did exactly the same—he simply came home.

"Wanna touch it again?" Bobby Ray pushed the bayonet toward me.

"Sure." I had never seen a bayonet before,

especially one taken off a dead Yankee in Kentucky. It was cold, hard, heavy, flecked with rust, though Bobby Ray tried to convince me that in actuality the rust was dried Yankee blood.

"My pa might ride down to fight with Emperor Maximilian's Frenchies in Mexico," Bobby Ray said. "I reckon I'll ride down with 'em, too. Kill me some greasers." He jerked the bayonet from my hand, almost cutting off a couple of my fingers. "With this!"

I blinked, stared at Bobby Ray, and then at my fingers, making sure that a rusty, dull bayonet had not removed any of my digits.

"Wanna come along with me?" He lowered his voice into a conspiratorial whisper.

"Huh?"

"To fight with Maximilian!" he shouted, forgetting the need for secrecy. "To get away from this Yankee rule! To slaughter Mexicans by the thousands, get us some *señoritas*, drink mescal. Have us a corker of a time. That's what Pa's a-plannin'!"

I tilted my head, then shook it. "Can't," I admitted.

"Why? You yeller?"

"No," I said. "I just can't leave Austin. I need to wait for Papa to return." Bobby Ray Pirkle frowned hard, which made me explain. "I mean, it just might be . . . well, that Papa . . . he'd like to go fight greasers down in Mexico with you and your pa and Maximilian, too."

Pulling off the towel he had wound around his neck, Bobby Ray Pirkle laid it on the verandah's floor, placed the bayonet atop it, and carefully wrapped it up. He looked at me with utter contempt.

"You is yeller." He shook his head. "And your daddy . . ." He snorted. "He ain't a-comin' back. Your pa's lyin' dead in some shallow grave in Virginy. Hogs is likely eatin' his flesh."

"That's a lie!" I said, jumping to my feet. "My papa's coming home. You just wait."

"Balderdash, Pierce. It's August, by thunder."

Bobby Ray Pirkle stood up, too. Luckily—for the both of us, I expect—the bayonet remained wrapped in a towel on the wooden floor.

"I say you're lying!" I told Bobby Ray.

"Prove it." He said that with a sneer.

I did. I belted the sorry cuss in his nose.

For the second time in my life, I got into a fight. My punch rocked Bobby Ray, who had been standing by the verandah's entrance, backward. Down he went, onto the grass, and I leaped atop him.

As I have said, he was three years my senior and he was taller, stronger, meaner than I ever could pray to be, but I had the element of surprise. Both of his hands covered his nose, and tears welled in his eyes. I even saw blood—definitely not rust—seeping between his fingers.

Mama always told me, when I was a few years

older, that my fuse burned slow, but when it exploded, watch out. She jokingly said that temper came from my Braden blood, not from hers, that the Pierces were always gentle souls. Grabbing a fistful of his thick hair, I jerked Bobby Ray's head up, then slammed it into the ground. Luckily the grass was thick.

"My pa . . ." I punched him again, but hit only his large arms that helped protect his face. "My pa . . ." Another punch. "He ain't . . . dead!" I hit him again. "You take . . . it . . . back." My knuckles were already scraped, yet fury blinded me to any pain. "Take it . . . back . . . I . . . say!"

I pulled back my fist, prepared to punch him again, but this time I felt myself being lifted off my combatant. Now it was me flying backward, landing on the grass, coming up to my knees, probably even shouting out a curse, and half expecting to find Uncle Moses Gage standing there, breaking up the fight, saving me from the moment when Bobby Ray Pirkle's senses returned and he realized that he could easily whip me.

It wasn't Uncle Moses, of course. It wasn't Grandpa Adair, or Grandma Beatrice, or even my mother.

It certainly wasn't my father.

No, far worse, Burt Pirkle stood there, his face a mask of rage, his body trembling with anger.

He reminded me of Hog Clagett from back in Jack County, Captain Earnhardt's hired hand who had survived a scalping during the big Comanche-Kiowa raid. Maybe you know the type, or have at least seen them in woodcuts in magazines and such.

Narrow-eyed. Tall. Bronzed. Leathery. Hard. Mean.

Burt Pirkle definitely had ridden with Terry's Texas Rangers. He had that look about him of a man who was born to ride a horse. Thin and gaunt, but far from weak. His body looked like a fence post, crooked, bent, yet unwavering. Beard stubble covered the lower half of his face, and I noticed his mangled right ear. His right hand had no pinky finger—not even a stub—and his clothes were filthy. No buttons remained on his gray shell jacket, which had been patched countless times and was missing the right sleeve. He wore boots, or what once had been boots, and spurs, and I saw a pistol stuck in his waistband.

For a moment, his blue eyes, icy cold, locked on mine, and then I heard the door to my grandparents' house open, as Grandpa Adair called out: "Burt Pickle, what in blazes is going on here?" Behind Grandpa's voice came the *ping* as Grandma Beatrice spit into her tin cup. Next I heard Mama's gasp. I guess Mama started down the front steps, but Grandpa must have stopped her.

Anyway, Burt Pirkle whirled away from me, and hoisted Bobby Ray to his feet. To my surprise, he slapped his son's head. "Boxed his ears," was how Grandpa remembered it a while later.

Down went Bobby Ray Pirkle to his knees. His father jerked him to his feet, and slapped him again.

"You call yourself a son of mine, boy?" Burt Pirkle yelled. "You call yourself a Pirkle!" He slapped him harder, and now Bobby Ray was crying. "Don't you whine, *you Mama's boy*." The last words came out mockingly, vilely, meant to shame his son, yet they also shamed me. Bobby Ray stood up, and Burt Pirkle kicked him in his hindquarters, booting him toward the street. "You can't even whup a puny cuss like Braden. An' I up an' give you that Yankee pig-sticker I won in . . . I taken off that dead bluebelly."

Bobby Ray took off, running for his home.

"Go on, boy!" his father called after him. "Go on. Run to your mammie. Run to your sisters. Squat to pee, why don't you! I'll be home directly. To get my razor strop an' wear out your hide."

When Burt Pirkle turned, I figured he would go after me now. Maybe even shoot me dead with that Colt stuck in his waistband. Instead, he walked to the verandah, where he stooped, knee joints popping, and retrieved the carefully wrapped bayonet. After he straightened up, he did not even look at me. Instead, he stared at my mother, then at my grandfather.

"Sorry to have disturbed you folks," he said, removing his hat with that crooked right hand of his, the one missing the pinky. "But don't you-all worry none. Us Pirkles won't trouble you-all no more."

The hat returned to his head, and his bowlegs carried him across the lawn, after which he turned down the street and walked away. To home, to whip and shame his son. Or maybe to the nearest grog shop. I prayed for the latter.

Only then, did Mama rush down the steps, run over to me, kneel, and pull me to her bosom.

"Them Pirkles!" I heard Grandma Beatrice say before she spit into her can and walked back inside.

Grandpa Adair muttered something a little more profane, and followed her into their home.

"What happened?" Mama asked.

I could not answer. I felt sorry for Bobby Ray Pirkle. I felt sick for what I had done. If I had held my temper, then Bobby Ray would not be in such trouble. I had learned an important lesson, one I never told my mother or grandmother, one I have never related until this moment as I write these words.

By Austin standards, the Pirkles were wealthy. By that I mean that they lived on the same street as Grandma and Grandpa, in a two-story home that had a barn and some acreage, with two Negro servants—slaves, actually, until Juneteenth. They were much, much richer than Mary Jane Clayton and her family. But now I knew, and had seen with my own eyes, the true definition of white trash.

CHAPTER FIVE

By the time September dawned, some things had returned to normal in Austin, much to the displeasure of boys and girls my age. Meaning that, school had opened. We had a new teacher, a young woman named Linda Ferdig with rosy cheeks and blonde hair worn in a bun. She was no Yankee. She spoke in a voice filled with a sugary accent, slow and Southern, more Alabama, Mama told us, than Texas or Louisiana.

Our new schoolmistress wasn't the only change. The Pirkles had moved. Truth is I saw neither Bobby Ray nor his daddy after that ugly incident in Grandpa and Grandma's front yard. Some say Burt Pirkle moved his family to Mexico, to join Jo Shelby or some other former Confederates. Others said the Pirkles went as far south as Brazil, where a number of colonies of *Confederadoes* were established. Another report said the Pirkles headed for Montana Territory to join the gold rush there. I had heard that Burt Pirkle had murdered a Negro, and was forced to flee to New Mexico Territory, and that his wife and family returned to Mrs. Pirkle's mother's farm outside of Jefferson.

The latter, I've come to believe, is half true. Burt Pirkle deserted his family, and took off for parts unknown—I don't think he killed a Negro, or anyone else—and merely disappeared, forcing his abandoned family to move to the Piney Woods.

✓ Back to our new school session. . . . Newcomers filled half the classroom, which seemed much smaller than it had during the war. Most of these newcomers were not the offspring of Yankee soldiers, nor were they the sons and daughters of Northern politicians sent to oversee the Reconstruction of Texas. Yet I feel certain that more than a handful of my new classmates came with carpetbaggers—Grandma Beatrice labeled almost all of them "grafters"—bent on cheating the last penny from the last honest citizen of Austin. If they had not been in Austin before or during the war, she did not trust them. Perhaps she had good reason.

Corruption ran rampant across Austin's halls of state, county, and city governments, courts and police departments.

On the other hand, as I child of nine years old, I paid scant attention to politics, criminality, and fraud, but focused on the three Rs Miss Ferdig taught in the classroom.

And I waited for Papa to come home.

One lazy Sunday after church in September, I sat in the family parlor trying to make heads or tails out of Alexandre Dumas, when someone tapped at the front door. Grandma Beatrice was out visiting a sick neighbor, so Grandpa Adair had decided this would be an opportune moment to catch up on the news at Harrigan's Saloon. So it was Mama who rose to answer the door.

"Keep reading," she said.

"I'll try," I muttered. Mama had told me that *The Three Musketeers* was full of sword fights and adventure, but I was having a hard time getting through a novel originally published in French and full of political maneuvering and foreign intrigue, although Porthos made me laugh. I pictured Papa when Athos was doing something interesting, and I sometimes fancied myself as D'Artagnan.

The door opened, and Mama gasped: "Oh, my God!" A noise followed that I could not make out.

I slammed shut the thick novel, leaped from my chair, and hurried into the foyer. The door remained open, and a rough-looking creature with a thick beard and worn boots held my mother in his filthy arms. Mama's head lay tilted back, and her arms dangled toward the floor.

"Let my mama down!" I shouted as I looked for something that I could use as a weapon. But I had no Yankee bayonet, courtesy of Burt Pirkle, to turn into a rapier, and my fists would do no harm to this thin but solid man who reeked of sweat and dirt and manure.

"Get some water, Pierce!" the vagabond said as he rushed past me into the parlor, Mama in his

68

arms where, appropriately enough, he laid her down on Grandma Beatrice's fainting couch.

Realizing that this stranger meant no harm, I hurried to the kitchen, poured a glass of water, and returned to find the man perched on his knees, fanning my mother's pale face with his battered gray hat.

I stopped in the doorway.

He saw me, kept fanning, and said: "You-all got any smelling salts around here?"

"I don't know," I answered.

His face was bronzed by the sun, which, combined with his thick, unkempt beard, made his blue eyes stand out like diamonds. He motioned for the water, so I brought him the glass, and stepped back.

"Lift your ma's head," he said.

I obeyed, and stupidly asked: "Is Mama alive?"

He sniggered. "Give her a shock, I reckon. Yeah, Pierce, she's alive. Just fainted."

Bringing the glass to her lips, he whispered: "Martha Jane? Martha Jane?" He tilted the glass just enough to wet her lips.

I could see Mama's eyes darting around underneath her slitted eyelids.

"Where's your grandma and grandpa?" the man asked.

"Out," I said, still waiting, praying for Mama to awaken.

He turned sharply. "You alone?"

I knew better than to tell the truth to a stranger, even one who knew both of our names.

"No, sir," I said, and thought up a lie real quick. "My pa just went out . . . to . . . to . . . fetch a newspaper." Quickly I looked out the window. "He . . . should be . . ."

The glass jerked up, spilling maybe a quarter of its contents on the front of Mama's blouse. For a moment the man's stark eyes looked practically human, and he said, in an urgent whisper: "Wil's home?" Followed by a shout: "Wil's home!" A heavy sigh escaped his mouth. "Thank the Lord for that."

Either the water on her chest or the man's shouting helped to revive Mama, whose eyes fluttered open slowly. The stranger looked back at her, and eased her up slightly.

"Martha Jane," he said softly.

Unlike me, she had recognized him immediately.

"Jacob," she said, but did not smile. "Is . . . Wil . . . with you?"

Uncle Jake did not seem offended that I didn't recognize or trust him at first.

Having recovered, Mama was sitting properly in the chair, directing my uncle to the decanter of brandy on the bookshelves. Uncle Jake sat on a stool I had fetched from the kitchen, since he refused to sit on any of our grandparents' nice furniture in his trail-worn duds.

70

"You didn't get my letters?" he asked Mama after taking a sip of the brandy and making a face. Peach brandy was not something he was used to drinking after four years of war.

"No. . . ." Tears welled in Mama's eyes, and mine, too.

"Wil . . . ?" Mama began.

His head shook. "I don't know, Martha Jane." He looked at me. "I don't know, Pierce. I wrote you-all from Virginia. Wrote my folks, too." He repeated his question: "Didn't you-all get my letters?"

Mama's head shook sadly. In those days, mail delivery proved to be a mighty poor gamble.

Uncle Jake sighed. "Captain Earnhardt?"

"He made it home," Mama said, and told him of the letter she had received from Gretchen and of the short note from the captain himself.

After another sip of brandy, Uncle Jake said: "Wil and I should've taken off with old Ben." He sighed. "I haven't seen Wil since I got captured."

That, Uncle Jake explained, had happened in March during the Petersburg siege.

A major supply depot practically spitting distance from the Confederate capital of Richmond, Petersburg was one of the longest battles of the war, certainly for Hood's Texas Brigade. It began in June of '64, although I'm not exactly certain when it started for Uncle Jake, Papa, and Captain Earnhardt. At first, the Yanks tried to cut the railroad lines, followed by a series of sorties, raids, even a few actual battles. Uncle Jake wasn't around when General Robert E. Lee finally gave up and abandoned the city, leaving Richmond to the Yanks, and heading toward destiny at Appomattox Court House.

"We were north of the James River," Uncle Jake explained. "Early October of 'Sixty-Four . . . maybe three, four days after Ben Earnhardt took the ankle express for home. General Lee wanted us to push the Yanks into the river, and we give it our best. 'Course, X Corps held that line, and those boys didn't have no quit in them. I don't know what happened exactly . . . one minute I was cutting loose with a Rebel yell, next thing I knew, some Yank was kicking me in the belly, and pressing a bayonet against my chest, telling me, that the war was over for me. I crawled out of the ditch I was in, and joined a mess of other boys bound for Point Lookout. That's where we spent the rest of the war."

He shuddered as he stared at his worn shoes. For the first time, I noticed those shoes were held together by filthy socks with rawhide wrapped over the soles and uppers.

"War was over for me? Not hardly. Be glad you never seen what all I saw at Point Lookout. Freezing half to death. Hunting rats to eat." He stopped, sipped the brandy again, and said: "Apologies, Martha Jane. You don't need to hear any of that."

Of course, that's what I really wanted to hear, but I bit my tongue.

"Was Wil . . . ?" Mama couldn't finish.

He shook his head. "We called that little fracas the Darbytown Raid. No, Martha Jane. The First Texas lost scores of men in that raid . . . including General Gregg. He knew no fear, General Gregg, none at all. He was leading us, waving that saber when he fell. Wil wasn't captured, and he wasn't killed."

He closed his eyes. "At least, not there."

"How . . . ?" Mama had to make herself ask: "How do you know?"

His smile held no humor. "Well, Point Lookout got to be quite the popular place for us boys in butternut and gray over the next months. More and more boys, including quite a few from the First Texas, arrived . . . seemed like every day. I always expected to see Wil. Must've been twenty thousand boys there by the time they made us take the oath and turned us loose. Anyway, Duncan Boone found me a month or two later. You don't know him. Neighbor of ours down in South Texas. Well, he told me Wil had survived the raid, said it took Sergeant Major Traywick . . . you don't know him, either . . . and two other boys to keep Wil from combing those grounds for my body. So he wasn't killed there. Not captured, either."

Another sip killed the brandy, and he set the glass on the desk. "Wasn't killed or captured at

Sailor's Creek, either, I learned from others, and General Lee lost I don't know how many captured and killed in that set-to. That one happened on April Sixth. Which, the way I figure it, means Wil was alive at Appomattox."

Mama rose, walked to Uncle Jake, and, lifting his hand, kissed it. "He's still alive," she said. "I know he's still alive."

" 'Course he is, Martha Jane," Uncle Jake said. "Wil Braden's too ornery to die."

Uncle Jake gave me the last brass button from what once had been his shell jacket. I treasured it more than any rusty bayonet, although I wished it had belonged to my father.

"Kept it all that time at Point Lookout," he said. "Traded the two others I had. Brass was good as gold sometimes in that pigsty. You keep it. You keep it, show it to your pa when he drags his sorry hide home at last."

He had cleaned up, bathed four or five times, shaved that rag-tag beard, cut and curried his hair, until he finally looked presentable. Grandpa Adair had bought him clothes proper for a gentleman, and, four days later, Uncle Jake decided it was time to return home to see his folks.

"If you get word from Wil . . . ," he told Mama, but did not finish.

"You do the same," she said before leaning over to kiss the pale cheek that had escaped the torment

74

of sun and wind for I didn't know how long.

For the time being, Jacob Braden walked out of our lives.

Grandma Beatrice had another thought. "Martha Jane, it's about time you and your son understood something. I don't like to say it . . ." She spit into her snuff can. "Don't like to say it at all." Of course, she did. "But Wil's dead. Dead and gone, probably in some forgotten field or ditch."

"Hush, woman," Grandpa Adair told her, but she didn't listen. She never really listened.

"Time to be practical," she said. "That's all I'm saying. Daughter, your man's dead. But you need to get on with the living."

"He's alive, Mother," Mama said.

A month later, I think even Mama had her doubts. Certainly I did.

Six months, and no word. She walked to the general store that served as our post office every day, and every day she came home with nothing. Yet she refused to accept Grandma Beatrice's advice, refused to believe that Wil Braden could be dead—even when we kept reading or hearing through the telegraph line known as gossip of many other men who would not be returning to their families.

How many of those wives and children had believed as Mama did, that their husbands, brothers, and fathers surely could not be among the hundreds of thousands of Confederate dead?

I attended school, I did my chores, I did my readings, and even practiced my arithmetic. I went to church on Sunday without complaint. I did not put up any fight when Grandma Beatrice cut my hair or had me take a bath. The way I figured things, if I were a good boy—really good—then God would reward me with Papa's return.

November 8, 1865. A Wednesday, cold, gray, and getting colder by the hour as a norther blew in. It is a day I will never forget.

Bundled up in coat, mittens, and scarves, I left school and trudged alone, head bent, back to the wind, wondering if Uncle Jacob had felt this cold when he had been a prisoner at Point Lookout. I reached into my coat pocket and squeezed the brass button I carried with me everywhere. In my imagination, I felt a tad warmer.

I hoped it would snow, but knew that it wouldn't. Rarely did snow touch Austin. Sleet and freezing rain, perhaps, but snow did not appear welcome. The wind moaned through the trees. No one walked with me. This wasn't like school in Jack County. Comanches and Kiowas did not raid this city, and the few friends I had at school lived on opposite sides of town.

Lost in my thoughts, I found my way home, which I entered through the back door, and then shed my boots and clothes. The house felt toasty, and I brought my empty lunch pail and sack of books into the kitchen, and immediately frowned.

Grandma Beatrice or Mama usually would have a cookie or sandwich and a glass of milk awaiting my return from Miss Ferdig's school, but I discovered the table empty.

"Pierce!" came Mama's voice from the family parlor.

"Coming," I said, and, stomach growling, I left the kitchen and found my way to the parlor.

Mama stood at a settee, truly smiling for the first time I think in years, and Grandma Beatrice sat on the fainting couch with her spit can held close to her lips. Grandpa Adair stood by the fireplace, trying to get green wood to catch.

In a rocking chair by the window sat a gaunt man with a ragged beard that would have made Uncle Jake's look like he had just stepped out of Austin's greatest tonsorial parlor. Crumbs from the cookie that was supposed to have been mine littered his beard. His filthy right hand gripped my glass of milk. His clothes looked to be nothing more than woolen rags, and, unlike Uncle Jake, he wore no brogans that belonged in a trash heap, but rather his feet were bare, and blackened. I looked at this creature whose hollow eyes and jaundiced face I scarcely remembered.

"Hello, Pierce," he said.

Yet even before William Lee Braden spoke those words, I was rushing to him, screaming—

"Papa!"—feeling the tears break loose like the norther screaming outside.

Papa deftly handed the glass of milk to Mama before I leaped into his arms. Thin, ragged, worn out, he was still solid, for the rocking chair barely moved as his dirty arms enveloped me.

"Too old for a kiss?" Papa asked.

"No . . . sir . . . ," I sobbed. He kissed my forehead, and set me down on the floor. "I'm a bit stove-up," he said, "for such horseplay right now." He brought up his big right hand, and tousled my hair. "What are you now, six?"

"Nine," I told him. "Almost ten."

He grunted, and took the milk, finished it, and handed the empty glass to Mama. "Ten," Papa said, and grunted again.

"Nine," Mama corrected. "He won't be ten until April."

Papa wet his lips. He stank worse than Uncle Jake had, which might have been why Grandma Beatrice remained on the fainting couch with her snuff can under her nose.

Grandpa Adair finally had the fire going, so he set the poker aside, and turned to face us.

Grandma Beatrice lowered the can long enough to say: "Ask them white trash Pirkles if that boy of yours fights like a nine-year-old."

"Mother," Mama admonished in a tight whisper.

"The Pirkles are gone," Grandpa Adair said, "and good riddance." He stepped away from the fireplace, bringing the refilled brandy decanter toward Papa, which he poured atop what remained of the goat's milk. "But Pierce here has been a fine boy, Wil. Big help to us all. Yes, sir. He's been a real top soldier."

Holding the brandy in his hand, Papa studied me. "Top soldier, eh?" he said.

Thus, my nickname was born.

CHAPTER SIX

How many times we filled and emptied the tub for Papa to bathe in, I don't know, but I recall hauling bucket after bucket of hot water and then doing it all again with the dirty water, which we lugged out into the bitter cold to use to water the oak trees in the backyard. While Mama, Grandpa Adair, and I worked at getting Papa thoroughly cleaned up, Grandma Beatrice cooked and cooked and cooked, and not just salt pork and beans, but stewed vegetables, beef from the butcher, and vinegar pie. By those days, we even had real coffee in Austin again.

It was when Papa was sitting on a stool, with a towel draped over his waist, waiting for the water to heat so he could shave, I first saw the round purple scar on his left shoulder. The bucket in my hand dropped to the floor. Papa started to chuckle at my clumsiness, but then he realized at what I was looking. He took a second towel and placed it over the scar, but not before I noticed another one, ragged, like a bolt of lightning had burned off the hair on his forearm and permanently scorched the skin. Seeing that, Papa sighed and shook his head.

"Medals," he said. Then, his tone turning tough, the way I vaguely recalled from before the war: "Best refill that bucket, Top Soldier. I ain't exactly clean yet."

"Pierce," Mama said. She was the one person who would never call me Top Soldier.

I obeyed.

Once Papa had shaved, the paleness of his lower face seemed funny that close to his bronzed cheeks, nose, and forehead. Even Grandpa chuckled over how Papa looked, but Mama nodded her appreciation and approval.

"I'll walk over to McKendry's mercantile," said Grandma Beatrice, finished with her cooking, "and buy you some new duds."

"Best let me take care of that," Papa said. "I've lost a smart of weight."

"Especially now that your beard's gone," Mama said, and patted Papa's shoulder.

"Yeah." Papa's eyes darkened.

"You got anything, Wil, other than Confederate script?" Even Grandpa Adair seemed to be in a joking mood.

"Yeah."

I felt I was the only one that noticed Papa's

tenseness. I wanted to say something to him, to let him know that I understood—although I did not, not in the slightest—but all that came out of my mouth was: "I'll go get the clothes for you, Papa."

"Stay here, Top Soldier." Papa pushed himself out of the rocker, and grabbed that waste of a hat. "Be back directly," he said.

"Wil?" Mama called out.

He did not answer, did not even turn around. He moved slowly, but with intense purpose. The door closed behind him, and my grandparents' home felt suddenly cold.

"What got into him?" Grandma Beatrice said to the closed door.

"The war," Mama answered softly.

"War's over," Grandma Beatrice said, and spit into her cuspidor. "I tell you, child," she told Mama, "many a time do I wish we'd stayed in North Carolina. You could have been married to Preston Truluck, could've given me a brood of young 'uns, including a granddaughter or two. . . ."

"Hush, Beatrice," Grandpa Adair said.

"He went out barefooted," I said softly, more to myself, not expecting anyone to hear, but Grandma Beatrice had heard.

"Catch his death if he ain't careful. Hard rock for a head, that pa of yours. Nothing like his brother Jacob. Why didn't you marry his brother, Martha? All that land the Bradens own down south . . . why . . . ?"

81

"That's enough, Beatrice," Grandpa Adair snapped, and my grandmother, for once, obeyed.

In the corner, I noticed the old Enfield Papa had carried off to war, the one Captain Earnhardt always said Papa had stolen from him. Maybe he'd give it to me. I wondered how many Yankees my father had killed with that beat-up weapon.

"You don't worry about your pa, Son." My grandfather stood beside me now, tousling my hair, while sneaking a peek through the curtain at the empty street. "Man who marched as long and as hard as Wil Braden done . . . man who probably footed it all the way from Virginia to Texas, he ain't gonna catch his death. Especially not as stubborn as he is, as all those Bradens are. Probably ain't used to being under a roof after six years in the Confederate Army."

Four years, I wanted to correct him, but, mindful of my elders, I just watched Mama silently ascend the staircase, and disappear into her bedroom.

I cannot say that things returned to normal. Now that I look back on those years, I am not certain if anything ever was normal. Papa spent the rest of November and all of December hanging around the house, building up strength. He slept a lot, and, mind you, this was a man who even I remembered would be drinking coffee before day broke, waiting for the sun to shed enough of its light so he could go outside and saddle his horse.

Oftentimes, he would be sleeping when I went to school, and when I returned home, he would still be in bed. The sleeping was one thing, but it was the silence that was uncomfortable. Papa had always been a taciturn man, but that reticence grew even more pronounced in Austin.

When he was awake, he sat in the parlor or on the front porch, rocking and chewing tobacco.

When he first got home, he had spoken some, asking a few questions, and explaining that he had written letters a few times, even posted them. When we said we had never gotten them, he apologized, though no blame could be attached to him for the incompetency of the letter carriers. He asked about Uncle Jake, and suggested we might travel south to see his family, but we knew that would not happen.

Not for a while, at least.

Papa remained weak. Not helpless, but he no longer was the solid Jack County rock that neither wind nor rain—nor Comanches or Kiowas— could erode.

"Do not worry about your father," Mama told me one night after our Bible reading. "He is fine. His strength will come back and we will return . . . soon."

"Return?" I asked. "Return where?"

She almost laughed. "Home, Pierce. Home."

Home. Jack County, Texas, and our hardscrabble

ranch. Return to the Earnhardts and Uncle Moses. I had almost forgotten all about that part of my young life.

"I bet that would make Papa feel better," I said.

"It would make us all feel better," Mama agreed.

The first Yankee soldiers had arrived in July, of course, and camped along Shoal Creek, but almost as soon as my father had come home, bluecoats came in by the thousands.

Sammy Donovan, two years my senior but one Reader behind me in our school lessons, showed up on my porch one Saturday afternoon with a great idea.

"Let's go to the madhouse," he said.

The madhouse, of course, was the Texas Blind Asylum, and it wasn't for crazy people, but the blind, and it hadn't been a school for the blind in years. Boys being boys, however, we all still called it the madhouse.

A beautiful building with towering white columns you'd find in some picture book about Greece, marble floors, and steps that weren't beginning to warp like those at my grandparents' house, the asylum had begun as the home for some man named Hill who was working on the state Capitol and other buildings in the 1850s. I guess this Hill gent was great at woodworking, but he didn't have much of a grasp on finances. He went broke, I think, and never lived in the home he had commissioned to be built a couple of miles outside of Austin.

So Hill leased the building to the state, and it became the Texas Blind Asylum about the time I was born. When a new building opened for the blind, the lieutenant governor lived in the fancy building. Grandpa Adair always said that that's when the home really became a madhouse. It became a hospital for Yankees, and a home for the commanding officer of the Reconstruction troops, and headquarters for the Yankees.

Sammy and I practically ran the two miles to the towering structure before slowing to a walk.

"You don't reckon the bluebellies'll shoot us, do you?" Sammy asked, losing his nerve.

"Let them try." Not moving quite as fast as Sammy, I let him remain in front of me. Until that afternoon, I had never been to the madhouse.

The grounds crawled with bluecoats, and smelled of horses. We stopped at the gate, and stared, mouths agape.

What raced through my mind was this thought: *No wonder we lost the war.* There must have been thousands of soldiers camped on the grounds, and no telling how many stood inside that massive two-story house. The Federal government had sent that many soldiers to Austin. The math astonished me.

"I don't see him," Sammy said.

"Who?"

"The general."

My mind raced. Grant? Sherman? Granger? Those were the only names of Union generals I could remember. I did not say anything, however, not wanting to show my ignorance. Instead, I leaned against the iron fence surrounding the complex, and tried to find someone who looked like a general.

The door to the asylum opened, but it was a woman who stepped out, dark-haired, thin, well-dressed. That's all I could tell about her. She was no general, but she looked straight at us, or so it seemed. When she turned, she began talking to one of the bluecoats.

"Hello, boys!"

The voice, while cheerful, caused me to bang my head against wrought iron, and Sammy Donovan spun around so fast, he tripped on his own shoelaces and fell to the damp, cold ground.

That caused a man in the road to laugh and the four hounds with him to howl.

"Don't shoot us, mister!" Sammy sang out.

Which caused the man to laugh harder and the beasts to bark even louder. The man, dressed in a blue coat and navy blue kepi, sank to the ground. The hounds turned their attention to him, licking his face, panting, barking. He hugged them all.

I wished I had dogs like that.

"Shoot you?" he said, and shook his head. When he told the dogs to stop, they did, two of them sitting at his feet, another lying on one side of him, and the fourth trotting on through the gate and toward the madhouse. "Are you foragers?" he asked.

We didn't answer.

"Murderers? Thieves? Deserters?" he pursued while scratching a bluetick's ears. He rose, saying: "I think you'll escape the firing squad. The gallows, though? I'm not certain. Come to see what a Yankee looks like, boys?"

I didn't expect a Yankee to look like him. He was no brute, no monster. Not handsome, not in my mind, anyway, but striking. Tall, but slight, fair-skinned, with a thick mustache, kepi tilted at a rakish angle, and blue eyes full of life. I thought he needed a haircut. Curly and blond, his hair stretched down to his shoulders, longer even than Grandma Beatrice's, although she arranged hers in a tight bun.

"Phil Sheridan," he said, and the dog lying in front of him rose quickly. The Yank nodded at us, and the dog walked toward us.

"You can pet him, boys. He won't bite."

Sammy Donovan was not about to move, but I swallowed down my fear, and kneeled, slowly extending my left hand, which the dog licked with his coarse tongue. I smiled, and patted the black and tan hound's head.

"Coonhound," the Yankee said. "Bought him in Hempstead. They called him Rip Ford, but I couldn't have a dog named that. Not after a fearless Texan Secesh, right?" He laughed. "Besides, he's a runt. Like Little Phil."

Sammy got up enough nerve to lift himself off the ground and pet the coonhound. The dog weighed maybe forty-five pounds soaking wet, indeed on the small side for a coonhound, but his coat was smooth and glossy, and he used his nose like a tool, sniffing Sammy Donovan all over. It must have tickled, because Sammy laughed. So did I.

The Yank rose, and I took the opportunity to study him more. The coat he wore had to have been tailor-made, with rows of spotless brass buttons stretching from collar to waist, and straps and golden epaulettes on its shoulders. The shoulder straps were what struck me as he bent forward to push himself to his feet. Trimmed with embroidered gold oak leaves, with two silver five-pointed stars on a field of blue.

This was . . . the . . . general. The spit dried instantly in my mouth.

"Autie . . . ," came a woman's voice.

The general, Sammy, and I turned at the pleasant voice, and the dogs leaped up, their tails wagging rapidly.

"Ah," said the general, "Libbie. Fear not, dearest bride, for these young vagabonds have sworn to me that they are neither looters nor freebooters. They do not plan to cross the river and join Maximilian in Mexico." He studied us, putting hands on his hips. "We might have to fight that scoundrel next, you know."

"They look like fine young men," the lady said. "Did you have a nice walk?"

"Walk?" The general slapped his thigh. "These hounds do not walk. They run. And I am famished. Gentlemen, if you shall excuse us. But come visit us, anytime, lads. The Army is always looking for good men." He brushed the dead grass off Sammy's backside, patted my head, and locked the lady's arm in his, escorting her toward the madhouse. When he whistled, the hounds followed him.

"That . . . was . . . him . . . ," Sammy Donovan managed.

"Yeah," I said, but had no idea who *him* was.

"Custer," he said.

Say what you will about George Armstrong Custer, most people in Austin did not despise him as a Yankee. Although he remained in Austin for no more than three or four months, most Texans seemed to respect him. The Yanks, I have been told, did not care much for him, for he was strict on discipline. Yet even Grandpa Adair said that General Custer treated law-abiding citizens in Austin with the utmost respect, and kept order in the city.

In February, he would be mustered out of the

volunteer Army, returning to his regular rank in the U.S. Army, and in a short time be promoted to lieutenant colonel of the 7th Cavalry. You know the rest of the story, I'm sure. Was he a glory hunter who led his men to death and destruction not quite eleven years after I met him, or a hero who died in battle? I don't know. All I know is that the George Custer I met briefly one time on a cold winter afternoon was full of life, had a beautiful wife, and really great dogs.

Bobby Ray Pirkle might have left Austin, along with the entire Pirkle clan, but Sammy Donovan and Mary Jane Clayton weren't my only classmates whose fathers had worn the gray. Other boys and girls in school—not the offspring of carpetbaggers—had fathers who had returned from the war. But at least three of my classmates were now fatherless, and many sons of soldiers regaled me with the daring wartime adventures of their dads.

Sammy Donovan showed us flattened Minié balls and the shoulder straps of a Yankee artillery major his pa had captured at Shiloh. Brett Andersen did even better, when he managed to sneak into the schoolhouse the regimental battle flag his father had bravely carried in the Battle at Bayou Bourbeau, wherever that was. The flag was musty, frayed, blackened by powder, and torn by bullets and grapeshot.

"It smells," Cynthia Reid said.

"Uhn-huh," Brett sang out. "Smells of . . . glory."

"What did your pa bring home, Pierce?" Cynthia asked.

"Oh," I said, trying to quickly think up a lie. "A revolver he took off a Yankee colonel. . . ." Then I prayed that a colonel outranked a major. "A medal." *Not enough,* I thought. *I should have said the brass button that Uncle Jake gave me . . . I hadn't even shown it to Papa yet . . . but how does one brass button compete against a battle flag?* Or maybe I saw the disbelief in my classmates' eyes, so one of Uncle Jake's stories raced through my memories, and I began.

"And General Gregg's saber. He was leading this . . . um . . . fracas . . . in Darbytown. General Gregg was, I mean. Not my pa. Papa was just a soldier, doing the real fighting. With my uncle. And lots of good Texans."

Saber? Why hadn't I just mentioned that Enfield rifle Papa still had?

Roland Gibbs, Grace Lynch, and Stan Evans moved closer. Even the carpetbagger kids seemed interested. My heart beat faster, trying to piece together what I remembered my uncle telling my mother.

"Anyway, General Gregg, he got shot. Shot dead. Leading the charge. But my pa, he saw the general fall, and he ran over to him, but there wasn't a thing to be done for General Gregg. Yanks got him in the heart. He was dead before he hit the ground. But Papa picked up the sword, and he yelled . . . 'Follow me, boys, follow me!' And they charged those Yankees. The Yanks, the cowards, skedaddled."

"And your father kept the sword?" Grace Lynch asked.

"Sure. Brought it home. To me."

"Why don't you bring it to school?" Sammy Donovan asked.

"And show it to us?" Stan Evans chimed in.

"No." My head shook sadly. "It's hanging over the mantel. Grandma and Grandpa wouldn't like it." I thought of something quickly. "And it's just a battered piece of Damascus steel." Damascus was a word I'd picked up out of a book I had been reading. Not that I knew what it meant, but I had heard of knives and swords being described as Damascus steel. "I mean, it's not like it's a battle flag." Someone, somehow had taught me about politics, I guess, for I knew I should butter up Brett Andersen and the others, those whose fathers had actually done something in the war. Or at least had been told about what had happened in what was now being referred to as "the recent unpleasantness" by Mama, Grandma Beatrice, and the ladies at church.

I continued: "Besides, my uncle, my uncle Jake, my pa's brother, he got captured in that fight.

Spent the rest of the war in a Yankee dung heap."

The one bit of truth I told.

"Pierce Braden!" Grace Lynch exclaimed. "Such language!"

"Thought you said the Yankees skedaddled," Roland Gibbs challenged.

Looking up, I discovered that all of my classmates, even Mary Jane Clayton, had come to hear my story. A few stared at the ground or the people walking down the streets, having no interest in some other tall tale of war, but most eyes were locked on me reverently. Which fueled my lies.

"They did. Still took prisoners, though. I mean, there was more to this fight than just that charge my pa led."

"Where is Darbytown, Master Braden?"

My mouth turned dry, and despite the crisp cold of December, I felt beads of sweat begin to form. Our schoolteacher, Miss Ferdig, had sneaked her way to eavesdrop on the whoppers I'd been telling my classmates.

"Ma'am?" I tried to stall for time.

Certainly Linda Ferdig was the youngest schoolteacher I had ever known. In fact, though I didn't know this until many years later, she was only fifteen years old in 1865, younger than students, Roland Gibbs or Penelope Alter. She had a round face, wore a gray winter dress, red scarf, and heavy shoes for the winter. I guess she was a good teacher, certainly fair, always impartial, and while she did not intimidate the way Mr. Lasater or Miss Madelyn could, and usually spoke to us gently—even when scolding Stan Evans or Dickie Walkup—those green eyes of her could bore into you like a drill.

Those eyes saw me for the liar I was.

"Darbytown," Miss Ferdig repeated. "What state is it in?"

"Why . . ."

Roland Gibbs sniggered, as if he had caught me in a lie. And he had. Well, Miss Linda Ferdig had, but Roland Gibbs had made a major error in judgment. His "why" had caused me to look away from our teacher and at him, and that was all I needed.

I answered: "Virginia, of course."

That had been a guess, albeit a good one. Almost every letter Papa had sent had been from Virginia, so chances were that the fight that had been Uncle Jake's last had occurred in the Old Dominion.

Something else Uncle Jake had said flashed in my brain. *We called that little fracas the Darbytown Raid.*

Miss Ferdig's smile and nod caused Roland Gibbs to loose his smirk.

"Indeed," our schoolteacher said. "Part of the Petersburg campaign. A tough loss for our brave men in gray."

We gaped at her. "My father," she explained, "had the honor to serve under General Longstreet. Come, children, recess is over."

Now, providing none of my classmates—or Miss Linda Ferdig—came to our home and looked at the mantel, I was safe. Or so I thought, until Miss Ferdig asked me to stay after school to wash the blackboard.

I didn't mind. She would never match Mr. Lasater as a teacher, but she wasn't bad, certainly more pleasant than that arithmetic-loving crone Miss Madelyn. Yet as soon as all of the children had departed, Miss Ferdig told me: "It is a sin to lie."

"Ma'am?" But my defenses shattered, my Adam's apple bobbed, and my head hung. "Yes, ma'am."

I expected a whipping—like the ones Mr. Lasater used to lay on Charley Conley—but instead her right hand fell on my shoulder. I stared at my brogans.

"My father took part in the Darbytown Raid," she said.

My head bobbed. "So did mine."

"I'm certain of that."

"And my uncle . . . Uncle Jake . . . Papa's brother, he did get catched by the Yanks."

"Captured," she corrected. "You know better than that, Pierce."

"Yes, ma'am." I thought of something else I had

said that had been true. "That general, named Gregg, he got killed, too."

"I know. I read about it in the *Weekly Democrat*. But your father didn't grab the fallen general's saber, did he?"

I didn't want to answer, and I didn't.

"Pierce." Keeping one hand on my shoulder, Miss Ferdig used her other to lift my chin, tilting my head until I had no choice but to look into her eyes.

"I don't know what he done!" I yelled. "He never says a thing about the dang' war!"

I hadn't meant to shout, but the anger just forced those words out. I wished Miss Ferdig would let me be, but her hand remained on my shoulder, and her eyes never lost any compassion. She wasn't angry with me, although she did correct my grammar.

"Can I finish my chores, ma'am?" I asked.

"Your father is a hero, as are all the brave men, young and old, who fought in that recent unpleasantness."

Then I realized just how angry I was . . . at my father. "Yeah, but Bobby Ray Pirkle's daddy brought him a bayonet. Brett's brought him that flag. Everybody who went off to that war came back with something. Even my uncle Jake gave me a button. I bet even Mary Jane's father brought something to show her, and all her pa did was guard Yankee prisoners at that camp in the Piney Woods."

"You wish your father had brought you a sword, Pierce?"

I shrugged. "Or something. Even a flattened musket ball."

"A sword is nothing, Pierce," she said. "Nor are used leaden bullets and balls, or revolvers, or articles of clothing torn off some enemy's coat. A flag used in war is nothing, either, not in the long run. Your father brought home something more valuable than that, Pierce." I blinked. She let go of my shoulder, and put both hands on her hips. Her voice lost its sweetness. "Do you think Grace Lynch, Ash Wilkerson, or Jeff Bonham want a battle flag or a saber?"

Grace's father had died of fever in Louisiana. Ash's had fallen at Corinth, Mississippi. Jeff's had been captured at Gettysburg, and apparently succumbed to disease in some prison camp.

"You have the greatest gift, Pierce. Don't ever forget that."

A gift, I thought with an unnerving amount of bitterness. A father who slept more than a newborn puppy, who seldom, if ever, spoke, and who wore ill-fitting store-bought duds and chewed twists of tobacco morning, noon, and night.

"Yes, ma'am," I said, and waited until Miss Linda Ferdig let me finish cleaning the blackboard.

Which was spotless, incredibly so, when school resumed the next morning.

CHAPTER SEVEN

Christmas came and passed without much fanfare, and 1866 dawned cold and gray, but full of people.

Back in November, our provisional governor, Mr. Hamilton, had issued a proclamation that said delegates for a constitutional convention would be elected January 8th, and that the convention would begin February 7th.

"Don't we have a constitution?" Mary Jane Clayton asked in school one morning, about the first time I had ever heard her speak in school.

"Sure," Roland Gibbs said. "It starts . . . 'We the people . . .'"

"That's the *Yankee* constitution!" Stan Evans roared.

"Class," Miss Ferdig said, and we settled down, a bit.

"There is the constitution of the . . . United States." It was still tough, even for a young teacher like Linda Ferdig, to come to terms with the fact that the Confederate States of America was no more. We were a defeated country. Her father, and other kin, had fought against that Constitution, and had lost.

"But states also have constitutions," she said.

"Didn't we have one already?" I asked. We had

been studying long division, and I had no desire to go back to that challenge.

"Yes. Now we need a new one."

"What for?" someone—I can't remember who—asked.

"Well," our teacher said, "there is the part about slaves that must be addressed."

We fell silent.

By that time, the 13th Amendment had already been added to the Constitution—the U.S. Constitution. We knew that, and knew slaves had been freed since last June, when that Yank general had sailed into Galveston with his troops and made known, in no uncertain terms, that all slaves were now free.

Reconstruction was a hard thing for us, no matter our age or where we were in our Readers, to grasp.

"As I understand it," Miss Ferdig said, "for Texas to be readmitted into the Union, we must have a constitution that denies the right of Secession, that abolishes slavery, that our debt incurred during the war be repudiated. . . ."

"What's that mean?" Dickie Walkup asked.

"Denied," she said. "It means the debt won't be paid."

Which sounded like math to most of us, so we did not question that part of the constitution further, fearing it would remind Miss Ferdig that some of us were supposed to be studying long division.

There were other items, Miss Ferdig told us, about state militias and the rights of our new black freedmen. (There would be other conventions, of course, other debates, before Reconstruction ended nine years after the war.) Then, she reminded us that we were studying math, and reluctantly we picked up our slates and chalk.

The convention began in early February, and basically became a fight between two groups, Unionists and Secessionists, and both groups were radicals. Little wonder Yankee and Republican control of our state would not end until 1874.

President Andrew Johnson had granted a general amnesty, so few Secessionists had been barred from voting across the state. That's why we had so many Secessionists in the constitutional delegation. One of them, I found on our front porch after school.

"Top Soldier," Papa greeted me, spit tobacco juice into the cuspidor between two rocking chairs, and gestured to the other tobacco-chewing rocker, "say hello to Captain Earnhardt."

Ben Earnhardt also spit.

The war had changed him, too, for he now wore a brown leather patch over his left eye, and a nasty scar sliced from his nose, through his graying beard, and just underneath his left ear. Otherwise, he remained as I remembered him—lean, leathery, hard as cedar. He stopped rocking, leaned forward, and held out a calloused right hand.

"Top Soldier, eh?" His piercing blue eye twinkled.

"Yes . . . sir." His grip almost crushed mine, and I winced, but neither he nor Papa noticed. When the vise let go, I stepped back, put both hands behind my back, and tried to massage, ever so discreetly, my right hand until the blood resumed its natural circulation.

"You remember me, boy?" Captain Earnhardt asked.

He wore tall black boots, and Grandma Beatrice would have had a cow had she seen the marks his big spurs were making on her porch. Striped britches, a fine silk shirt, burgundy waistcoat, black cravat, and a porkpie hat. His linen duster lay draped over the porch railing.

"Yes, sir," I replied. "How's Clarke?"

He frowned. "Fine."

"Tell him I said howdy."

He looked away from me. "Yeah."

"And Uncle Moses?" I asked.

That lightened the captain's face. He rocked back in the chair, and grinned, but only briefly. "Same old Moses. Ain't uppity . . . like some of them boys is gettin'." Dismissing me, he turned to Papa and asked: "You heard about that Freedmen's Bureau, Wil?"

A month or so before the war's end, Congress—the U.S. Congress, I mean—had established the Bureau of Refugees, Freedmen, and Abandoned

Lands, which practically everybody shortened to the Freedmen's Bureau. Part of the U.S. Army, the agency's main function was to provide relief to citizens, black and white, left homeless from the war. I guess it also had to deal with lands abandoned by the Confederacy or confiscated by the Union. The bureau established schools and protected the rights of the newly freed slaves. I saw nothing wrong with that, but Ben Earnhardt did.

"Just more Yankees kickin' dirt in our faces." He spit.

"You running for office, Ben?" Papa asked.

"No," he answered, and cut loose with a few oaths. "And I sure didn't want this job, but . . ."

The screen door opened, but Mama stayed in the doorway. "Pierce," she said, "we need some kindling chopped, then do your school lessons before supper." I nodded again at Captain Earnhardt, picked up my satchel and dinner pail, and Mama held the door open for me as I walked inside.

"Ben Earnhardt," she ordered, "take off those blasted spurs."

Over dinner, Grandpa Adair, Papa, and Captain Earnhardt—but mostly Grandpa and the captain—talked about Jack County, the country, and cattle. For Mama's, and Grandma Beatrice's, and perhaps, my sake, they did not go into much detail in telling stories about the Elm Creek Raid and the scalping of Hog Clagett, and they did not even bring up Yorker Nott's death.

The captain did point to the Enfield rifle, cleaned now, and leaning in the corner near a coat rack. "See you still got that ol' Enfield rifle you stole from me."

Papa laughed. I hoped that would lead to war stories, but the captain asked: "When are you-all comin' home?"

"Soon," Mama said wistfully. "I hope."

That caused both of my grandparents to frown.

Papa said: "No point . . . in the winter."

"Reckon not," Captain Earnhardt said. "Been cold up north. Northers comin' in as regular as a two-dollar watch."

Mama stood, refilled the China cups with real chicory coffee.

"Spring," Captain Earnhardt said after Mama had finished her chore, "of course, has its own problems."

To which Papa merely nodded.

"Everybody along Lost Creek'll help you, Wil," Captain Earnhardt said.

Papa nodded again. Still standing in front of the side table and facing the wall, Mama said: "You've already done plenty, Ben."

"Not me," he said, shaking his head. "Mostly Moses Gage, Clagett, Morrell, and the boys. I was off on some fool's errand playin' soldier boy.

With Wil here." He shook his head at some old memory, grinned slightly, and for a moment, I thought Ben Earnhardt might share some memory of the war, regale us with some story of honor and glory and bullets and bayonets—something Papa never would do—but to my disappointment, all he did was ask: "You seen Jacob?"

Papa just shook his head. The cup looked like some dollhouse toy in his big hands, but he only looked at the lukewarm coffee, not drinking it.

"He came by," Mama said, turning. I tried not to notice the redness in her eyes. She wanted to go home. I knew it.

But Papa . . . ?

"Got here before Wil did," Mama said, and sat back down in her chair. "It was good to see Jacob. It is great to see you. Jacob went home to Harrisburg."

"Only been there once," Captain Earnhardt said, just to say something. "When we joined up with the First Texas. Remember that, Wil?"

Papa smiled weakly, but said nothing.

The captain raised his cup. "To Hood's First Texas."

Their cups and my glass of water clinked, but the stories ended with the toast.

Captain Earnhardt, Papa, and Grandpa Adair retired to the porch to smoke cigars or chew tobacco and talk about cattle and the constitutional convention, or the weather, or anything—

anything except the late war. Mama, Grandma Beatrice, and I did the dishes. Then it was off to bed and our nightly reading from the Bible, before Mama tucked me in—though I felt too old for such nonsense—with a kiss on my forehead.

"Mama?" I asked when she reached the door before heading back downstairs.

"Yes, Pierce."

"Does Papa not want to go home?"

She came back to me, kneeled by the side of the bed, and put her hand on my heart. "Of course he does. But winter's no time to move with all we have to do."

That's when something Uncle Moses had said rang through my brain, and I shivered.

Pierce, you ain't got no home to go back to.

Captain Earnhardt had been seeing to our stock, probably branding our calves, but Indians had destroyed our place on Lost Creek. I also knew what Ben Earnhardt had meant when he had said that spring had its own sorts of problems. Not northers, although they could certainly wield an icy grip on northern Texas at that time of year, but Comanches and Kiowas.

The Constitutional Convention of 1866 began on February 7th and lasted until April 2nd. Secession was deemed illegal, the war debt was "repudiated," and freedmen were free, of course, although the new constitution prohibited blacks from holding

105

public office. The new constitution would not rid us of Yankee rule, however, which is why there would be other constitutional conventions in the years to come, although Ben Earnhardt would serve on none of those delegations, having had his fill of politics, at least, until after Reconstruction.

He dined with us a few evenings during those months, but those conversations revealed little or held much interest for a boy fast approaching ten years old. Certainly I heard no war stories.

Still Captain Earnhardt's arrival brought one major change.

Papa began getting up before dawn. Usually he was stoking the fires and getting the coffee boiling. He didn't say much as I ate breakfast, but he was at the table, drinking coffee and reading the morning papers, and when I came home from school one February afternoon, I did not find my father sitting on the front porch, rocking and chewing tobacco.

"Where's Papa?" I asked Mama.

She smiled. "Working."

He had landed a job at Daniel Manning's livery stable, working mostly with mules, and soon began shoeing horses and mules. He had always been a pretty good farrier—most ranchers in northwestern Texas had to be. When he left Manning's livery, he joined Bill Cogburn's group of carpenters. Most ranchers in northwestern Texas had to be fair to middling carpenters, too. A lot of construction had started up in Austin, and Papa would come home bone-tired.

Tan skin replaced the whiteness where his beard had been, and he began to grow a mustache. He put on weight. Muscles hardened his arms, his legs.

He didn't talk much—well, he never had—but he brought a new glow to Mama's face. The sorrowful look faded, and her eyes beamed.

Of course, I hoped this papa, more like the father I remembered in Jack County, might talk about some battle, some act of heroism. I didn't even need my father to be the hero. I just wanted to hear . . . something. Something like the stories Sammy Donovan, Roland Gibbs, and Brett Andersen told me about their fathers. Even if they were exaggerations. Even if they were outright lies.

Papa would ask me how school was, nod at my answer, or give me a chore to do. That was about it. Dickie Walkup once told me that he gone fishing with his pa at Shoal Creek. My father had never taken me fishing.

On April 11th, a Wednesday—I remember because I was now ten years old—I came home to find Grandma Beatrice crying.

My first thought was that Grandpa Adair had died from an apoplexy, but he stood in the corner of the parlor talking quietly with Papa.

After blowing her nose, Grandma Adair shook her head, and pointed at my mother. "Did you know this, Daughter?"

Mama sighed. I looked up at her. "It's our home, Mother," Mama said.

"Full of savages and black-hearts," my grandmother said, and I sucked in a breath.

Now I understood why Papa had been working so hard. Earning money. I understood something else. I would be leaving school. Not that I minded Miss Ferdig any more, but I had always feared that Brett Andersen or Sammy Donovan or someone would drop by my house and see that no saber hung over our mantel.

Grandma sniffled, shook her head, spit into her cuspidor, and turned toward Papa.

"When are you-all leaving us?"

"Monday," he answered.

We were leaving Austin. Returning to Lost Creek. Going home.

PART II
1866–1869

CHAPTER EIGHT

Going home had to be the best birthday present of my life, although I would have to wait five days—sitting in school for two of them. School, of course, did get me out of some of the packing, yet truthfully we had little to bring back to Jack County.

Luckily I managed to escape Austin without any of my classmates coming over to see that captured saber that did not hang over the mantel. Good byes on that last day of school lacked emotion. Miss Ferdig merely shook my hand and wished me well back home in Jack County. By the spring of 1866, I guess, farewells had become all too common. Many families were always uprooting, trying to get away from Yankee rule, or setting out for adventure in wild-sounding frontiers like New Mexico Territory, Arizona Territory, Colorado Territory, Mexico. We were just heading some two hundred fifty miles north and slightly west, and staying in Texas. Besides, who would really miss the Bradens in Austin—other than my grand-parents?

Grandpa Adair shook my hand, and Grandma Beatrice kissed me full on the lips—she tasted just like snuff—and they watched us pull away, Papa's Enfield rifle beside him, Grandma Beatrice's old

111

pie safe—a present she wanted us to have—wrapped in the back of a rickety old covered wagon pulled by two stout mules, one blind in one eye.

We followed what would soon become known as the Great Texas Cattle Trail, during that era of long trail drives to the Kansas railheads. The year we left Austin, cattlemen had begun trailing longhorns north to Missouri on the Sedalia or Shawnee Trail, but we saw no herds.

Travel went slowly, to Temple, then to Waco, where we had to wait a day before we could cross the Brazos River on a ferry. A massive suspension bridge, which would use some three million bricks, would go up in three years, making the crossing less harrowing but just as expensive because of the tolls charged.

Finally, after ten or eleven days, we reached Fort Worth, where we spent several nights sleeping in a wagon yard before lighting out for those last sixty miles on a straight northwestward route to Jacksboro. The travel would have been easy, but Papa did not want to go alone, so we waited to hitch along with a wagon train bringing grain and supplies through Jacksboro on the way to Fort Belknap.

Spring always arrived early in Texas. May was warm, the grass already green, and a half moon seemed a safer time to travel.

"Indians up Jack County way?" Papa asked the

burly man with an unkempt red beard who ran the wagon yard.

"Peaceable of late," the big man answered, "but you know how Comanch' and Kiowas get."

"Criminy, Jasper," said the thin, toothless gent mucking the stalls, "they's peaceable up that way 'cause there ain't nothin' left for 'em bucks to plunder no more."

"Shut up, Zane," the big man snapped, and surreptitiously tilted his head toward Mama and me.

On the 7th of May, we left Fort Worth on the Fort Belknap Road through Decatur, and arrived in Jacksboro four and a half days later, eating the dust of the oxen, horses, and freight wagons.

I can't say I recognized Jacksboro.

Pigs and dogs ran loose in the streets, and more than a few buildings had been boarded up, abandoned. Across from the town square lay the business district, mostly vacant lots and shacks that a norther could likely blow down. The streets were rough—dusty when dry, a bog after a rain storm. Still, the town seemed bigger and crowded as the wagon train moved along toward the livery stable and mercantile on the western side of town.

Papa reined in the mules in front of the hotel. As soon as he set the brake and climbed down into the muddy street, a figure appeared in the open hotel doorway.

"Wil Braden," a man's voice drawled, "ain't you a sight for sore eyes."

Papa turned, and stepped up onto the boardwalk, which was almost as muddy as the street, as a rawhide-looking man in a big black hat stepped out into the light.

"You a hostler now?" Papa asked as he shook the hand of the tall man.

"Just checkin' to see if Capt'n got any letters . . . ," said the man who seemed familiar, but I just couldn't place him. Then something caught his attention, and he walked out a few steps to stare down the street. Sitting in the wagon with Mama, I followed his gaze as Papa stepped to the man's side.

"Look at 'em, Wil," the man said as he jutted his jaw at a rider on a worn-out mare riding in from the west. "Men like him's been driftin' in for months now." He spit a river of tobacco juice into the mud at our mules' hoofs. "Ain't much to look at, is he, Wil?"

"He has a horse," Papa said in good humor. "More than I got."

"Gotta take your word for it," the man said, "that *that's* a horse."

The rider was gaunt and jaundiced, wearing bib-and-brace overalls, but no shirt, a ragged bandanna, and only one boot, the left—if even you could call it a boot. His right foot was bare, black with grime. The mare looked in even worse shape than the rider, with it ribs protruding. The rider wore a wide-brimmed gray hat, with a chunk of brass, stamped **C.S.A.**, pinning up the hat's front brim.

This man was no cleaner, no filthier than Uncle Jake or Papa had been when they first returned home from the East.

I heard Papa tell the man in the black hat: "Once we were paroled, the Yanks made the officers pool their horses. Draw lots for a mount. 'Course, Yanks being Yanks, they'd pick the best horses for their own . . . if they could find any decent mounts by that time." That might have been the most I had ever heard Papa speak of the late war.

The man in the black hat looked at our mules, and shifted the quid in his cheek. "Them what you drawed, Wil?" he asked.

Papa's head shook. "Those are the best I could buy in Austin. I didn't get any horse in Virginia. I wasn't an officer. But I was infantry. Used to walking." He tilted his head as the stranger on the skeletal horse made his way toward the Palo Pinto Saloon. "You recognize him?"

"Nah. Comin' in from the west now. Might've gotten lost. You?"

"He wasn't with Hood's First Texas," Papa said, and when they turned toward Mama and me, I studied the man's features, still trying to recognize him.

His eyes were brilliant and blue, his face

115

bronzed beneath the beard stubble that was stained from the tobacco juice dripping down his chin. He wore a blue and white checked shirt tucked into buckskin trousers that in turn were stuffed inside scuffed boots. The rowels of his spurs were huge. A big Bowie knife was sheathed on his left hip; on his right, a holster held a Navy Colt. Deerskin gloves were tucked inside the brown belt that held his weapons, and a yellow bandanna was tied tightly against his throat. He looked to be a dangerous man, but he smiled as he saw me for the first time, and lifted that long arm toward me.

"That ain't your boy, is it?" he asked.

"That's Top Soldier," Papa said.

The man remembered his manners, and quickly lifted his black hat. That's when I recognized him, although the last time I had seen him, he had borne no ugly scar across the top of his head. Some people did survive scalpings, and Hog Clagett stood before us as living, breathing proof.

With his hat on, you couldn't tell he had been mutilated, for his curly, graying dark hair looked normal where it hung down toward his ears. Hair grew from the back of his head, too, but the top bore what looked to be raw, scarred skin. From a distance, I imagine, Clagett would have looked just like some fellow who had gone bald, but up close—and Mama and I were close—it looked as if someone had just yanked out the hair from the top of his head. I guess that's pretty much what had happened.

"Missus Braden," he said humbly, and even bowed, revealing just how horribly scarred his head had become. "Welcome home, ma'am."

My stomach heaved, but nothing came up my throat.

"Eldon." Mama never called him Hog.

I shook his hand, but could not help staring as he held his hat at his side. Mama scolded me for my rudeness, but Hog Clagett merely laughed.

"It don't bother me, ma'am," he said, and started to don his hat again. "I'm used to it."

I blurted out: "Did it hurt?"

Chuckling, he settled the big hat on his head, saying: "It hurt like a son-of- . . ."

Mama interrupted his curse, and Clagett laughed again.

Papa's eyes held that mischievous glitter as he pointed inside the open doorway, saying: "You want to get checked in, Martha?"

That startled me so much that I quit gawking at Hog Clagett. My mouth was open, but no words came out. Mama gave me her smile that told me I would not like what I would soon hear.

Papa and Hog Clagett began to wander off, leaving me on the mud-caked boardwalk with my mother.

"We shall stay here a while," she informed me.

"But I thought we were going home."

Her head bobbed. "'And so, after he had patiently endured, he obtained the promise,'" she quoted, then waited.

I guessed: "John." I usually guessed John.

Her head now shook. "Hebrews," she corrected. "Chapter Six."

"The promise is home," she said. "But not now."

I knew why. Seeing Hog Clagett had reminded me, and now those words Uncle Moses Gage had told me before we had been shipped off to Austin and Grandma and Grandpa rang through my mind once more. Yes, I would have to endure.

That night, as we supped at a café on the eastern edge of town—the meals at the hotel being more than we could afford—Mama broke the rest of the news to me.

For the next few weeks, Papa would be gone again, trying to get the ranch in some semblance of shape, but he would visit us in town as often as possible. Eventually we would return to our ranch, but first there would be school.

Mr. Lasater's schoolhouse had been six miles from our ranch on a relatively well-traveled road, about halfway between home and Jacksboro, convenient, more or less, for ranch kids and some town students. But that school had been established when Jacksboro was nothing more than a few buildings. Now that town had grown, though it was a far cry from a thriving metropolis, a new school had been built on its eastern edge.

Our teacher was Miss Linda Riley—yes, another teacher named Linda—a tall, gangly creature with her hair in a braided bun and a wart on the tip of her nose, but she wasn't the first person I saw on my first day back in school. The first was Charley Conley.

He had shot up and filled out. I still remembered him as that big brute who kept our teachers busy just with whipping him. He still remembered me from jamming that chicken bone in his ear and causing Uncle Moses to embarrass him in front of all the others.

"Well," he said, as he pounded some things that looked like white-coated black bricks, behind the schoolhouse, a one-room stone building with small, glassless windows on the sides. "The yellow runt is back in Jack County." Chalk dust covered his homespun clothes.

"Charley," I said meekly, and looked around. The yard was empty. I began to hate my mother for making me go to school early on my first day.

"I ain't yellow," I said, "and I ain't no runt." I couldn't back down, even though Charley's arms looked about as big as Uncle Moses's.

"No?" He beat two of those black things together viciously before dropping them into a bucket. "You and your ma runned off to Austin. Couldn't hack no Injuns."

My mouth opened, but quickly shut. I remembered his sister, kidnapped and held by Indians years ago—until Uncle Moses had bought her release—and I remembered his mother, who had been killed in that raid.

"Cat got your tongue?" he chided.

I looked back toward town, but no other children had appeared.

"Well?"

"No," I said. "Where's Miss . . . ?" I had forgotten our teacher's name.

He cursed our teacher, cursed me, and threw two of the black bricks at my feet. "Clean 'em," he ordered.

They might make good weapons, I thought, lacking any chicken bone at the moment, so I picked them up. He laughed as I stared at the things in my hands.

Back when Mr. Lasater taught school here, and even in Austin, we had always cleaned our black-boards and slates with wet rags.

"What are these?" I asked.

"Erasers, you dunce." He spit between my legs. "Some Yankee invented 'em a few years back. We got us a chalkboard, too, and slatin' paint. Teacher's a Yank, you know."

Something appeared in the corner of my eye, and I turned, hoping to find Mama or Uncle Moses or maybe even Papa—better yet, Uncle Jake—but no. My heart sank.

"Who are you?" the newcomer asked.

"Hi, Nancy," I said, not answering her question.

Nancy Livermore. Still tall, still in pigtails, still with those hazel eyes. Still two years older than me, and already having forgotten my name and the fact that once she had liked me, kissed me full on the lips, even though I had slapped her for some slight.

"It's the yellow-livered runt," Charley Conley said, "Pierce Braden."

"Ahhhh." She set down her lunch pail and sack of books, and looked me up, then down, and at my lunch pail and empty sack. "Top Soldier." Her hazel eyes gleamed.

"Huh?" Charley Conley said.

I couldn't believe it. How had Nancy Livermore heard the nickname I'd been given by my father and Grandpa Adair?

Trying to ignore both of my classmates, I slammed the erasers together as hard as Charley Conley had been doing, hoping that I might vanish in a cloud of dust from the slating paint.

"He's a real Top Soldier," Nancy said, and it struck me that her mother had been chatting with my mother. Then I remembered something. Nancy's father owned a saloon in town, and Hog Clagett was known to frequent that bucket of blood. Hog Clagett had to be the big-mouthed culprit.

As Nancy Livermore told Charley everything, I kept looking at the back door, hoping Miss

Riley—I'd finally recalled her name—would come to my rescue.

When Charley Conley moved, I stopped pounding the erasers. He stood six inches taller than me, and he was barefooted. I wore brogans, since Mama wanted me to make a good first impression at school. I also wore britches, not just a long shirt.

"Top Soldier!" Charley scoffed. "He ain't no soldier at all."

"It's just a name, you two," I said. "I didn't pick it. I didn't pick Braden, either, and I sure didn't ask to be saddled with Pierce."

Nancy stepped back, and her eyes lost that gleam, that bit of wickedness. Maybe she had detected something in my voice, something that even eluded me, and certainly escaped Charley Conley's feeble intuition.

Charley jerked both erasers from my chalk-covered hands, and examined them as if he were inspecting a musket. I heard voices and footsteps behind me and knew that other children were arriving at school. Charley had been waiting for an audience. Now he had one.

"Top Soldier?" He laughed. "Well, I reckon we'll find out, won't we, Pierce Braden, the yellow-livered runt who run off to hide out the war in Austin?"

"I got no quarrel with you, Charley," I told him.

"Well, I got one with you," he said. " 'Cause I ain't never forgotten that night at Capt'n Earnhardt's."

Both erasers slammed into my ears and they felt like bricks. Stars and that white dust blinded my vision, and then it felt like a mule kicked me in the stomach, because down I went, onto my knees, coughing, heaving, gasping. Next, my lips split, my teeth ached, and I tasted chalk and dirt and my own bile.

"Kill 'em! Kill 'em, Charley!" My classmates—Charley's audience—cheered him on, but I did not detect Nancy Livermore's voice among them. Not that I could hear much of anything.

I lay on my back, still unable to see, but I could taste something in my mouth, something other than gall and blood.

Chalk! Charley was ramming one of the erasers into my mouth.

"Miss Riley! Miss Riley! Come quick!"

My brain was registering Nancy's voice screaming for help.

The eraser was now being used to pound my nose. Blood streamed down my face.

So this was my third fight. I had—sort of by default—won my first one, thanks to Uncle Moses's timely interruption, and had definitely whipped Bobby Ray Pirkle, but Charley Conley had exacted revenge. Likely he would have killed me, as he pounded my face and head with the erasers he held while sitting on my stomach, crushing me with his enormous weight. I got ready to die.

But, just like that first go at fisticuffs with Charley Conley, and just like that fight in the front yard by the verandah with Bobby Ray Pirkle, someone intervened. Charley Conley flew off my side, and what followed was a loud slap.

CHAPTER NINE

"Stay there, Charles Conley!" a voice shrieked. "As God is my witness, if you even move I will skin your hide!"

Someone helped me up. I vomited.

A moment later, I felt myself being pulled into gentle arms, a gentle bosom that I was covering with chalk dust and blood.

"There, there, child," this woman's voice told me. "Everything will be all right. Are you injured badly?"

Are you kidding me? I wanted to say. I had been beaten to a pulp, my nose broken, my lips busted, and several teeth loosened. In that first fight all those years ago, I had no front permanent teeth. Now I feared I might lose a couple of permanent ones.

"I'm . . . f-f-fine," I managed to say, wiping my lips and nose with the ripped sleeve of a shirt Mama had just bought a day earlier at the mercantile. Then that Braden blood flowed through me, and I made myself push away from the comfort. "I'm fine," I declared. And through the blood, I made out a thin, rectangular face, blue eyes, and a wart—just before I sank into a river of blackness.

Inside the schoolhouse, I came to. *Great,* I thought. *My first trip into the school, and I've been carried inside, unconscious.*

The students must have cleared Miss Riley's desk because I found myself stretched atop it. Nancy Livermore and Jesse Kendrick stood by my head, one fanning me with a McGuffey's Reader, the other holding a wet rag against my nose. When I tried to sit up, someone else's hand pushed me down.

"Lie still, Master Braden."

Despite the wart, Miss Riley was not an ugly woman. Plain maybe, and thin as a rail. Her eyes were gentle, but that hand that held me down on her desk had a strength that her bony arms belied.

She smiled—her teeth were perfect—but those blue eyes remained lined with concern. "I have sent . . ."

Panic laced my voice when I said: "You haven't sent for my mother!"

"The doctor," she informed me. "I have taught boys long enough to know better than fetch their mothers after a fight."

"I don't need a doctor, either," I said.

When Doc Köhler showed up, Miss Riley

hustled my classmates to the front of the building, while the sawbones adjusted his spectacles and stared down at me. He was a big man, with a full beard, furrowed brow, and a soggy, well-chewed, unlit cigar stub that his yellow teeth continued to shred as he went to work, after rolling up his sleeves. His name was German, but he spoke without a trace of an accent—on those rare times when he actually spoke more than a grunt or a curse.

There was no gentleness to him, but he never apologized, not even when I screamed when he applied what felt like horse liniment soaked in chile peppers on my cuts, not even when I let out a swear word when he set my broken nose.

At last, he handed me a fresh wet rag to wipe my face, then he turned toward my classmates, removing the wet piece of a cigar from his mouth. "Who did this?" he asked, removing tobacco flakes from his mouth.

"Me!" Charley Conley pushed aside two boys younger than me, and moved to the aisle, hands on both hips.

I made myself sit up, and swung my weak legs so that they hung down.

"Come here!" The big German pointed to a crack in the floor maybe a foot from where he stood.

Charley obeyed, and, as soon as he looked up, Köhler knocked the smirk off Charley's face, dropping him to the floor.

"Doctor Köhler!" Miss Riley screamed, while the students gasped.

The German was not listening to Miss Riley. He stretched a beefy finger down into Charley Conley's stunned face. Blood seeped from one of the big brute's nostrils, and tears appeared in his eyes. I almost smiled.

"If your father were . . . !" the doctor thundered.

Yet Charley Conley cut him off, and his words tore through me so much that I went from hating that bully to feeling pity for him.

"My pa's dead!" Charley shouted. "He died at Chickamauga. And I don't even know where that is or where he's buried!"

The doc's finger was still in Charley's face, but the big man said nothing. He seemed frozen, until Miss Riley said softly: "It's in Georgia, Charley, practically on the Tennessee border."

The doctor stood upright, placing the cigar stub back between his teeth, and taking the rag from my hand and returning it and all his other medical items into his black satchel. He adjusted his eye-glasses, put on his bell crown hat, and handed mc a tincture. For pain, I guess. He didn't say anything until he reached Miss Riley.

"No charge, teacher," he said, tipped his hat, then maneuvered through the children, closing the door behind him.

I made myself get off that desk, and began returning Miss Riley's books and things to what I figured might be their proper places. I couldn't look at Charley Conley, whose father I never knew. But I remembered the Jack County Seven, those brave men who, under their elected captain, Conn Conley, had marched south to join the other Texans who would comprise Hood's Texas Brigade. Seven men had left. Only Ben Earnhardt and Papa had returned.

A few students began to help me. I heard the door open and close, but I didn't turn. Soon I became aware that Miss Riley was standing next to me.

"Take your seat, Master Braden," she said, pointing to a desk next to a freckle-faced blond-headed boy.

"Yes, ma'am," I said, leaving the tincture on the desk.

Charley Conley had left, which made the rest of my first day at school fairly passable—until I had to go back to the hotel and face Mama.

Mama said: " '. . . but whosoever shall smite thee on thy right cheek, turn to him the other also.' " She peeled back the bandage over my nose and, frowning, waited for my reply.

I didn't even have to guess John. "Matthew," I said. "But Charley Conley . . ."

"Hush with Charley Conley." She wadded up the bandage the big doctor had applied to my busted nose, and dipped a clean one in some sort of concoction she had brewed in the wash basin of our hotel room. "Your first day of school. One ruined shirt. One scarred face."

My spirits brightened at the thought of scars marking my face for life. "You think so?"

"Pierce."

I considered myself chastised, staring at the rug on the floor. I managed to mumble: "He started it. I didn't do nothing."

She corrected me. "Didn't do anything."

"Yes, ma'am."

The bandage went back over my nose. It stank. As Mama stepped away, she stared, murmuring: "I suppose we can't blame Charles Conley, the poor child."

"I can blame him," I snapped, having briefly forgotten the pity I had felt for him earlier that morning in school.

Mama didn't seem to hear. She walked across the room, where she pulled back the curtain and looked down upon the main street of Jacksboro. Papa was at our ranch, or what remained of it, and would not return until Sunday.

"Was Papa at Chickamauga?" I asked.

She didn't seem to hear me, perhaps because my voice was nasally, so I repeated my question.

"Where's that?" she said.

"Tennessee. No, Georgia . . . but near Tennessee. They fought there. In the fall of 'Sixty-Three."

Miss Riley had been forced to abandon her

course plan for a short history lesson on the Battle of Chickamauga.

Mama's head bobbed. "I don't know." She kept looking out the window.

"Did he know Mister Conley?"

She turned, and I could tell she had been crying—over me, I guess, the wayward son who had spoiled his first day at school, and his looks, and his new store-bought duds. "Yes." She waited, maybe trying to find the right words. "I knew his wife." She smiled sadly. "She was such a sweet woman." Then she turned back toward the window.

"Papa would've fought there, too, I guess," I said.

It seemed an eternity before she spoke again. "Probably. Only by then, letters from your father were scarce."

"I reckon I could ask him."

"You know he wouldn't answer."

"Why not?"

Mama left the window to sit on the bed at my side. She turned sad eyes on me, and said: "My baby brother used to ask Grandpa Timothy about the Revolutionary War. He fought in it, Grandpa Timothy, as a very young man. A big battle took place at Guilford Courthouse, not far from where we grew up. Grandpa Timothy was always reluctant to talk about it . . . probably because he was a Tory . . . but he always told Charles . . . ' 'Tis not a place to which I desire to return.' Wil . . . your father . . . feels the same."

"I don't want Papa to go back to Chickamauga or anywhere in Virginia, Mama," I told her, slightly insulted because I felt as though she must have thought I was being callous.

"That is not what Grandpa Timothy meant, Pierce." She tapped her skull. "Or Wil."

At ten years old, I could be quite dense, but slowly an understanding came to me. "Oh." I pouted a bit, then asked: "What's a Tory?"

She took a deep breath, and slowly exhaled. "Well, during the Revolutionary War, not all Americans . . . I guess they would have been called colonists then . . . wanted to be independent. They did not all fight against the Crown. Those that chose to stay under King George's rule were branded Loyalists, or Tories. 'Twas not a pleasant place to be . . . North Carolina . . . in those times."

That left me fretting. I had never realized that not everyone wanted independence. "You mean he was a . . ."

Her look stopped me. Smiling, she said: "Tory or Patriot. Rebel or Yankee. Who is to say who was right and who was wrong? Both sides thought they were right."

I touched the bandage, which I could no longer smell, with the tips of my scratched fingers. "I just wish Papa would tell me some story about the war . . . ," I muttered.

"I know. But he never was much for talk, Pierce. Charles . . . he never understood Grandpa Timothy's reticence, either. Charlie . . ." Suddenly Mama's tears flowed freely, and she sobbed: "Oh, how I miss Charlie."

"Charley Conley?" I cried out.

"Goodness, no," she finally managed to say. "Charlie was . . ." She pressed her lips together, and then I knew.

Charles Pierce, the uncle who died not far from here before I was even born. The one killed in 1858 while hunting with his favorite dogs on West Keechi Creek.

"I'm sorry, Mama," I said.

Her tears had stopped. "It's all right, Pierce," she said, and she pulled me close to her. "You would have liked him. He was wild, crazy, knew no fear. Jacob, your uncle, reminds me so much of Charlie."

"Why didn't you marry him then?" I said.

She laughed again. "I didn't know Jacob. . . ." This made her laugh. She couldn't seem to stop even as she got up to find a handkerchief in one of the drawers. "That," she finally said, "did not come out as I had intended. I did not know Jacob. I did not love him. I married the right Braden."

The Bible lay atop the dresser from which she had gotten the handkerchief. She picked it up and said: "Now . . . it is bedtime. We shall read from . . . John." She smiled at me. "And I trust you will forgo any fisticuffs with Charley Conley at school tomorrow."

There would be no more schoolyard fights with Charley Conley, for he never returned to Miss Riley's schoolhouse.

There would be no more hotel, either. Hotel rooms cost money. So when Papa—who studied my injuries but made no comment—returned to town, we gathered our things and put them in the wagon and moved ourselves to a vacant lot in what folks called "Rat Row." That's because the buildings, most of them little more than shacks, housed more rats than people. We would sleep in the back of the wagon, do our cooking on a campfire, and live, basically, like squatters. Which I guess is what we were, like those rats, if only temporarily so.

It would have seemed like a grand adventure, except my classmates made fun of me. They had shingle roofs and stone houses. I had a canvas roof and a wagon box. They had privies. We had to use the public one behind the livery.

Mama said: " 'It is better to dwell in a corner of the housetop, than with a brawling woman in a wide house.' "

I responded: "Proverbs."

She kissed me on the cheek. I hadn't guessed John, but I had guessed right, though I'd almost said Psalms.

• • •

Of all the teachers I had, Linda Riley did the impossible. First, I had never dreamed that I would like any of my educators more than Mr. Lasater, but Miss Riley—despite that wart that always drew my attention—topped my first teacher. Now, neither she nor her abacas helped improve my math skills, but she introduced me to a subject that I would grow to love even more than reading.

At first, I sat up front with the younger kids— the Abecedarians, as they were called, because their primary task was to learn their ABCs. Soon, however, Miss Riley realized I knew my ABCs and could read better than some of the big kids, so I found myself shuffled further back on the boys' side of the aisle. I was directly across from Nancy Livermore, still two years my senior, on the girls' side of the aisle. Jealous of my accomplishment, Nancy quickly forgot that she had ever liked me.

School let out for the summer on the first Monday of June, not to resume until the first Monday of September, so I had less than a month with Miss Riley, who hailed from Rhode Island— perhaps from the same town where chalk erasers had been invented. She did not just teach us reading, writing, and arithmetic. There were two weeks remaining in our session, when she brought out a book that inspired me.

"Class," she announced, "close your Readers. I want to teach you something that's near and dear to my heart. Geology."

"What's that?" Bobby Weatherly asked.

"What do you see on my desk?" she asked.

We all looked, but Nancy Livermore was the first to answer. "Rocks."

"We can learn about Earth by reading rocks," she said, which caused all of us to giggle.

That she had expected, so she went to the desk, and picked up a rock, and then began walking up the aisle until she stopped and placed the rock in Nancy Livermore's hand.

"What can you tell from this rock?" she asked.

"That it's dirty." Nancy quickly dropped the rock on her desktop, and wiped her hands on her dress.

Even I laughed, until the rock suddenly fell into my hands.

"And you, Master Braden?"

Bobby Weatherly sang out: "It's just a chunk of coal."

I knew better, since it was in my hands. It wasn't dirty, either, just black. "It's not from around here," I said.

Bobby Weatherly would not shut up. "How would you know? You ain't even from here."

"I was born here, you dumb . . ."

"Master Braden," Miss Riley said gently, and I frowned. "Go on. About the rock, not Master Weatherly."

"It's black," I began.

"Flint!" Jim Fountain yelled out. "Injuns use it to make arrowheads. Used to, anyhow. Before we learnt 'em 'bout iron."

My head shook. "No," I said before Miss Riley could correct Jim Fountain's grammar. "Flint's hard. This . . . this is full of . . . little holes." I looked up and guessed. "By water?"

She smiled, and took the rock from my hand. "A good guess," she said.

A good guess, but wrong.

"Those holes came from air," Miss Riley explained. "Or gas. From heat. Very, very intense heat, for at one time this piece of black rock . . . which we call lava . . . was molten, flowing, red-hot lava from a volcano."

That got everyone's attention.

The piece of lava was passed around, and Miss Riley returned to her desk and started to pull out a book from the row of titles on her desk, but changed her mind, and instead arranged the books on their sides. The books tipped and slid, forming layers.

"The layers of the rock," she said, pointing at the books. "The layers of the earth."

Next she pulled out one of the books, and came down the aisle, stopping beside my desk. "This is an old book, perhaps," she said, "but one I still admire, although the author's *The Wonders of Geology* is probably better suited for classroom studies. But we shall start with this." She handed me the book.

Peter Parley's Wonders of the Earth, Sea, and Sky by Samuel Griswold Goodrich.

"Read, Master Braden," she said, and so I began.

Miss Riley showed us many examples of rocks and fossils, the latter being a new discovery for me, as well as wooden models that illustrated geological formations such as mineral veins and seams of coal, first introduced in England back when Texas had been a republic and not a state.

Seriously I doubt if I would have become a miner if not for Mr. Thomas Sopwith, inventor of those models, or Miss Riley, but certainly I would have not followed this pursuit if not for Mr. Goodrich and his book first published in 1840.

Yet it wasn't rocks that drew me to geology. It was the dinosaurs—Plesiosaurus, the wing-fingered Pterodactyl, the Dodo, the American Tapir—and wonders such as geysers and volcanoes—Vesuvius, Etna, Skaptar Jokull—and basaltic rocks, the Hot Springs of Reykium, icebergs, whales, and the fiery center of the Earth.

I don't know if Miss Riley would have been called a catastrophist, uniformitarian, or scriptural geologist. More or less, she let us make up our own minds during the few days we studied fossils and bones and the differences in rocks. She also let me take *Peter Parley's Wonders of the Earth, Sea, and Sky* home with me.

Mama didn't cotton to it—dinosaurs not being in the Bible—but she let me read Goodrich just the same.

Miss Linda Riley and Samuel G. Goodrich opened another world to me at ten years of age, and it fascinated me. Before school let out, she would give me another book, an 1863 edition of *Text-Book of Geology* by James D. Dana, LL.D. Mama liked that book even less that *Peter Parley*.

Those books would almost make me forget about the late War Between the States, my father's rôle in it, and Hood's 1st Texas. Peter Parley would send me out one Saturday afternoon in search of a rock or fossil—some sort of present that I could give Miss Riley on the last day of school.

That errand almost got Uncle Moses and me killed.

CHAPTER TEN

Uncle Moses had ridden into Jacksboro early that Saturday morning just as Mama and I were returning from the mercantile, where Mama had bought some food. He came to town on a big black horse—Moses Gage was known far and wide for breaking some of the best mounts in the county—pulling a smaller dun mare, saddled, on a lead rope. In front of the abandoned building next to our vacant lot, the big freedman swung down, wrapped the reins around a rail, removed his wide-brimmed straw hat, and bowed graciously at Mama as he stepped onto the boardwalk.

"Missus Braden," he said warmly as he returned the hat atop his freshly cut hair.

"Moses Gage." She curtseyed. "You have not aged one bit."

He grinned. "Hard to tell, I reckon, ma'am, me bein' as old as Methuselah." His big right hand jutted toward me. "Howdy, Top Soldier."

I felt like Mama. He had not aged, and looked just as I had remembered him. Solid as a stone wall, graying stubble covering his face, dressed in a dirty collarless shirt and probably the same buckskin trousers he had worn the last time I'd seen him. His boots were worn, and his spurs chimed. His holster held an ancient Walker Colt—a revolver most men would have carried on their saddle, not their hip—and, sheathed on his left side, a big Bowie knife with a brass D-ring handle that helped balance the massive .44.

There was no way to hide my pleasure as I shook his hand.

Until he asked: "What happened to you?"

Instinctively my hand reached up toward my bandaged, busted nose.

"You been fightin' again, Top Soldier?"

It seemed as if everyone now knew me by that nickname.

His voice lowered as he caught Mama's hard stare. "You whup up on that Conley boy again?"

"Moses . . . ," Mama chided.

He straightened, still grinning, and pointed at the dun mare, which was slaking its thirst in a water trough beside the big black. "Your pa thought maybe you'd like to go for a ride this morn, Top Soldier."

Staring at the horse, I tried to recall the last time I had been in a saddle. "Papa!" I shouted. "Papa said that . . . ?"

"Well . . ."—he rubbed the beard stubble on his chin—"not in so many words, I reckon, but . . ."

So it had been Uncle Moses's idea. Mama tried to change the subject.

"How is the ranch?" she asked.

"Comin' along. Take a while. But we'll have you-all helpin' us come a week or so after Top Soldier gets his educatin' done."

"Can I go, Mama?" I begged. "Ride with Uncle Moses."

She nodded. "Get a hat and some clothes more suitable for riding," she told me, and turned to Uncle Moses. "How long will you be gone?"

"We'll just ride up toward Salt Creek or so. Few hours, ma'am, if that be all right with you."

I was already in the back of the wagon, rifling through the gunny sack that held my clothes.

"Gee willikers!" Uncle Moses reined in the big black and stared at me in disbelief. "Your teacher, that Miss Linda, she's a lady, ain't she, not a dog?" I grinned. Moses shook that big head. "And you want to give her a bone?"

I was already reaching into the saddlebag, pulling out Samuel Griswold Goodrich, and thumbing through the pages until I found what I guessed might be the best illustration. I held *Peter Parley's Wonders of the Earth, Sea, and Sky*, and Uncle Moses leaned in the saddle and stared, first at the book, then at me.

"I ain't never seen nothin' like that in all my days. And certainly not in these parts."

"It's a palaeotherium," I said.

"You want the whole shebang?" He pushed back the slouch hat. "A whole skeleton."

"No. Of course not, though that'd be something. Any dinosaur bone'll do. In fact, this French guy named Cuvier, he was the first to discover this dinosaur, and all he found was a tooth."

"A tooth?"

My head bobbed.

"A tooth'd be a whole lot easier to find than that thing," Uncle Moses said, pointing at the illustration, and shaking his head.

I closed the book, and slipped it back into the saddlebag. A pterodactyl would probably be out of the question, too.

"Dinosaur," Uncle Moses said, shaking his head. Then he kicked the black into a walk, and I nudged along the mare, which I had named Linda Ferdig Riley Lasater, after my favorite teachers. Miss Madelyn Cox did not fill that bill.

"Some years back," Uncle Moses said thoughtfully, "this Tonkawa told me he found some big tracks down along the Paluxy. Never seen the like, he said. Three-toed things, made from what looked to be like some giant bird."

I had no idea what kind of dinosaur that could have been. Pterodactyl? Dodo? Or maybe the Tonk had been lying.

"I even rode down there with that Injun. Was just before the war broke out. Didn't see nothin', though. Talked to a gent who had started a gristmill. He didn't know nothin', hadn't seen nothin'. Tonk swore he wasn't lyin', though. But the Paluxy had flooded since he'd seen them three-toed tracks." He stretched out his hands. "Huge. Huge they was. Not no dove or quail, or even an eagle. The Tonk figured the flood had covered the tracks, and guessed it'd take another big flood to uncover 'em." He whistled. "Would've like to have seen 'em tracks, though."

"Where's the Paluxy?" I asked.

He chuckled. "Too far to get you back home in a couple of hours." He pointed in a general direction, more south than east. "Four days' ride, I reckon, but there ain't been no big floods of late.

Coyot' bone we might find, even a tooth. But I don't know about no . . . what'd you call that thing?"

"Palaeotherium."

"That's a mouthful."

"Maybe a fossil, then, instead of a bone."

He chuckled. "Figured some flowers would suit a lady teacher more'n no dinosaur bone."

We were fording a sea of Indian paintbrush and black-eyed Susans, the wildflowers coming up to the dun mare's knees. On one side of the road, a small bluff, the closest thing that passed for a mountain, sprang up from the prairie, while on the other side stood a deep and dense thicket.

I considered the bluff, thinking about layers and geologic things. If only we lived closer to the Paluxy, I thought, deciding my chances of finding a dinosaur bone were quite miniscule. "A creek-bed would likely work," I told Uncle Moses. "I can look for a fossil."

"What exactly is a fossil?"

I tried to come up with a proper definition, when Uncle Moses did something he rarely did. He cursed.

Quickly he reined in his black, and motioned me to do the same. As I pulled up beside him, he wet his chapped lips with his tongue. "Master Pierce," he began, and I knew he had spotted something serious because his face had turned rock-hard, and he wasn't calling me by that nickname any more. "I want you to do just like I tell you. Pull that carbine out of the scabbard, and butt it against your thigh."

He was already doing the same with his long gun. Mine was a Spencer repeater, which weighed slightly less than a Howitzer. I struggled at first, but once I had the walnut stock resting on my thigh, I thought I might be able to keep it there, though I needed both hands to do it. My reins I dropped across the mare's neck, and hoped she would not bolt, just graze on the red and yellow flowers.

Uncle Moses's Sharps was much heavier than the Spencer, but he had no trouble keeping it steady on his thigh with one hand. His other held the reins to the black.

"Just do exactly like I tell you," he said, staring ahead at something I did not see. "Don't run. Don't scream. Don't . . ."

I started to protest. But then I saw them.

Most of them from either side of the bluff, but quite a few just appeared as if summoned from the Earth's bowels by a wizard. They rode at us at a gallop.

"My . . ." I had to stop, to grab the reins, as Linda Ferdig Riley Lasater raised her head and started to turn.

"Don't run!" Uncle Moses shouted. "Run and we're both dead."

I had no intention of running, but the dun had

other plans. It took both hands—one of which held the Spencer carbine—but I tugged hard, and spoke in short bursts, and the dun danced a bit before she settled down. By then, the riders had slowed their mounts to a walk. In a matter of seconds, they formed a semicircle around us.

"Bring the carbine back up," Uncle Moses said, "but gently. Don't point it at nothin' but sky."

I no longer smelled the wildflowers, just vermilion and sweat, but mostly my own fear.

Before us sat roughly two dozen warriors in Comanche and Kiowa saddles, eyes black, feathers dancing in the wind. Some held lances, and a few brandished war clubs or revolvers. Most held rifles. Scalps dangled from some of the lances.

Uncle Moses barked something in a tongue I had never heard, more of a grunt than a word, but one of the Indians responded. Neither Moses Gage nor the Comanche sounded friendly. I tried to swallow but the inside of my mouth had turned into desert sand.

"They're not wearing paint," Uncle Moses whispered to me in English, and then said something else in the guttural tongue.

He was right, of course. None of their faces had been painted for war. They still looked fierce, though, and deadly.

The one talking wore a bonnet of what appeared to be hundreds of eagle's feathers. He had been the first I had noticed, because when he had that high-stepping coal-black stallion at a gallop, the headdress spread out, as if it were an eagle in full flight. He was short—what I might even have called fat—but imposing. Rings of large brass hoops hung from his ears, and the braids of his shiny black hair had been wrapped in otter skins. He wore no shirt, but scars pockmarked his copper chest, and a bear claw necklace dangled from his neck. His leggings, breechclout, and moccasins were unadorned. He held a lance, but no scalps hung from it. Instead, the eight-foot spear with an iron blade possibly a foot long had been draped with deer hide and turkey feathers.

Next to him, on a black-and-white pinto, sat a sober-looking man with gray hair hanging beneath a buffalo headdress. Though also short and stocky, he looked as if he had been riding horses all his life. In fact, every one of the Indians might have been born in the saddle. But this one was different than all the others, because a ragged gray mustache drooped over his mouth all the way to his chin. The others bore no facial hair. I had never seen an Indian with facial hair. Not that I'd seen many Indians, of course, and never Comanche and Kiowa warriors.

He said nothing. He didn't even blink. He just stared.

To his right, a young Indian—scarcely older than me—kicked his sorrel into a walk toward us. The Indian with the headdress of eagle feathers stopped his conversation with Uncle Moses to watch as the boy eased his sorrel next to my dun. The boy wore no feathers in his hair, not even a headband, and carried just a quiver of arrows and a long bow. The breechclout, leggings, and moccasins were Kiowa, Uncle Moses later told me, but his shirt was blue calico.

Only briefly did he look at me, studying the Spencer held rigidly against my thigh, before he leaned over in the saddle. Linda Ferdig Riley Lasater turned her head, and snorted, but I gripped the reins and urged her to behave.

Peter Parley's Wonders of the Earth, Sea, and Sky had been carelessly stuffed into the saddle-bag, which I had not fastened, and now the young Indian reached over and pulled out Goodrich's book. He slipped the bow over his shoulder and hefted the book for weight, then shook it, the pages fluttering in the wind. Finally he held it open, eyes filled with a curiosity. Then suddenly he stopped and shouted something.

The Indian with all the eagle feathers frowned. The one in the buffalo headdress did nothing. A few spoke among themselves before one brave kicked his pony into a walk and pulled alongside the boy with my book. Then three others moved out of the semicircle to look at the book. I didn't know what to do, so I just sat in the saddle, the reins and the carbine in my clammy hands, and watched.

One of the older braves with a battered old flintlock reached for the book, but the young one whipped it back, barked something that led the others to laugh. The one with the flintlock spoke sharply, but then quickly tugged the hackamore on his pinto and rode back into the line. The others followed suit, and rode back into position. When the one with my book started to take his place alongside the sour-faced, mustachioed Indian, Uncle Moses shouted: "*Keta!*"

The boy stopped the sorrel, and turned to stare at Uncle Moses, who was looking at me.

"Don't let him ride off with that book," Uncle Moses said.

Uncomprehending, I blinked. Did he want me to shoot down that Comanche for taking *Peter Parley*? With a Spencer carbine? And then just wait for the other Indians to kill us?

"He'll think you're weak," Uncle Moses said to me. "A coward. Make him trade something for the book."

"But I want my book back," I whined.

"Pierce!" Uncle Moses's voice had turned icy. "You want that book? Or you want to die?" He jerked his head toward the waiting young Kiowa. "Go."

After I wet my lips, I nudged the dun forward, careful not to drop the heavy carbine I held braced against my leg. The dun responded as if she knew what I expected, and stopped when I was alongside the young Indian with Goodrich's book. I thought about grinning, just to show him that I was friendly and that this was not my idea, but his face chilled me.

I didn't get mad. I swallowed down what little spit I had managed to form in my mouth, and tilted my head at *Peter Parley*. Knowing no Comanche or Kiowa, I meekly said: "Trade."

The brave looked at the older warriors in front of him, and then past me, settling his eyes on Uncle Moses.

"*Narumuuru.*" Moses spoke Comanche, he later told me, as the Kiowa tongue was too difficult to understand, and was sung more than spoken.

But the young boy understood, and he frowned before glancing at the leader, the rider with those eagle feathers, whose head bobbed. He might have even smiled. The one in the buffalo headdress sure didn't.

Frowning, the young Kiowa looked around. Finally he reached to his side, and whipped out a knife, studied it briefly, then thrust it, handle first, toward me.

The handle came from an antler, wrapped in a dirty, dark hide. The blade was dark, well worn, but I could tell that it had been honed to a keen edge. Reluctantly, after lowering the reins across the mare's neck again, I took the knife, and held it as if I didn't know what to do with it.

That caused the brave to say something else,

which prompted a few chuckles from some of the other riders, and the next thing I knew, the young warrior was handing me a fringed, beaded sheath. So I took it, and dropped both knife and sheath into the saddlebag.

"Trade!" he said in English firmly, nodding his approval, and moving back into line.

"Just stay put for a while," Uncle Moses said, and he kicked his horse forward, moving a few feet until he was close to the one with the eagle headdress. Then he slipped the Sharps into the scabbard, but he made sure the Indians could still see the big Walker on his hip. Like me, he draped the reins over his horse's neck, and began carrying on a conversation with the one I assumed was the chief.

They spoke with their hands, not words.

Fascinated, but not understanding, I watched. They talked like this, with just a few grunts or words, for a good five minutes. Then, without a word or even an indication, the Indians turned their mounts and galloped back across the prairie toward the bluff. When they vanished, Uncle Moses pulled the Sharps back from its scabbard, and stared at the dust and crushed wildflowers. He sat there for a long time, until, satisfied, he eased from the saddle, still holding the carbine, and sank onto his haunches.

"Oh, Lordy."

I dismounted, and as soon as my boots were on

the ground, my knees buckled, and I crashed beside him, causing my dun mare to side-step a bit before she settled down and returned her attention to eating Indian paintbrush.

"You all right?" Uncle Moses asked.

I nodded. My innards had begun to roil. Moses Gage looked incredibly old and feeble.

"Best not . . ." He stopped to knock off his hat, and wipe his face with the calico bandanna. "Best not . . ." It took him a third try to get it out. "Best not tell your ma, or your pa, 'bout this. Least not . . . no . . . don't never mention it. To nobody."

My head bobbed, but I remembered the knife and sheath.

"How do I explain . . . ?" I couldn't finish, either. Another thought struck me. "The book?"

"You losted it."

Which wasn't quite a lie.

"Don't reckon we'll find no dinosaur bones today, Top Soldier," he said, still wiping his face, which glistened with sweat. "No fossils, neither."

We fell silent. After a moment, he rose to fetch his canteen, guzzled down about half of the water, and pitched it to me. I drank, too, wiped my mouth, and asked: "Why didn't they kill us?"

He shrugged. "Old colored man with short, kinky hair like me. Youngster like you. No glory in it, I reckon. And they wasn't painted for war. Just huntin'."

"You speak Comanche?"

"Enough to get by. The Kiowa . . . the young buck you traded with . . . he savvies that lingo. Most Kiowas do. Kiowas, they be smarter than Comanch'. Met one up in the Nations oncet who could also savvy Spanish, French, even some Latin. Well, that's what ol' Satanta tol' me. I don't speak no French, certainly no Latin, and not much of that Mex lingo. Anyway, I done most of the talkin' with signs."

Moses was speaking, I figured, to keep from shaking.

"I watched," I told him.

"You made a good trade," Uncle Moses said, reaching again for the canteen.

I tried to think. The book had been a gift. Miss Riley had told me she didn't want it back, and I had the other book, too, Dana's *Text-Book of Geology*, since our geology studies had ended. Miss Riley had even said the latter was a better book for learning. But the knife and the sheath? How would I explain that to Mama? I sure couldn't hide it in a covered wagon.

"The knife . . . ," I reminded him.

Uncle Moses had emptied the canteen. "Oh," he said, his head bobbing. "Right. Tell your ma . . . no, I ain't teachin' you to lie to your elders. Say a friendly Indian traded it to . . . no, that won't pass muster with your pa. Give it to me." It took a lot of effort to stand, and even more to

152

walk to the mare, and pull the beautiful sheath and the ugly knife from the saddlebags. I half stumbled back to Uncle Moses, and gave him the knife, which he deftly slid into the sheath.

Immediately he handed the sheathed knife back to me.

"Tell 'em I give it to you. Ain't no lie," he said. "I just done gived it to you."

CHAPTER ELEVEN

We decided not to go looking for fossils or dinosaur bones, but we did not rush back to Jacksboro, either. Instead, Uncle Moses and I kept our horses at a walk, turning to look over our backs a lot. The Comanches and Kiowas did not return to take our scalps.

I tried to count my blessings. Had Papa been with me, instead of Uncle Moses, or had Mama decided to ride along with us, we could all be dead, our scalps hanging from one of those lances. I had lost *Peter Parley*, but I still had Dana's *TextBook of Geology* in the back of the wagon in town. And I had a Comanche knife and fringed sheath. For our lives and a book . . . yes, I guess I had made a pretty good trade, after all.

"What did that boy want with a book?" I blurted out when we stopped to let our horses drink from a stream.

Uncle Moses said: "Reckon maybe he wants to learn about dinosaurs and fossils and such."

"You mean he can read?"

Laughing, Uncle Moses shook his head, and said: "Top Soldier, I'm just funnin' you." He seemed to have fully recovered from our brush with death. He shook his head. "Most likely, that buck'll just rip that book apart, stuff it in the next shield he makes. Won't stop a bullet, but might deflect an arrow or some such." He winked. "And those drawin's of the dinosaurs and other critters, he probably figures that'll give him big medicine."

When school let out, Papa returned to Jacksboro again and escorted Mama and me home. That's when school really began, for while Papa had accomplished much in the few number of weeks—digging a new well and filling in the old one; putting up a corral; making a lean-to; tearing down the ruins of our barn and home— much work remained. And we took to it.

Most of the chimney stood, but little else, and our first priority was our home. So Papa would hitch the two mules to the wagon, and we would leave Mama at home while we rode to the limestone quarry to get stones for our new home. When we had enough stones to go with those Papa had salvaged from our first house, we went to work.

First, we repaired the chimney, and made a new

154

hearth. That's when I discovered my first fossil imbedded in a nice flat limestone.

"Mama!" I said after understanding what I had found. "Come see!"

Sweating over a hot fire, she stood up, wiped her forehead, and asked: "What is it?"

"It's a fossil!"

She sighed, started to go back to work, but must have decided to investigate, and she came over to the hearth, looking as though every bone in her body ached. Papa arrived with another stone a few minutes later to find Mama and me studying the brick.

"What's so fascinating?" he asked.

Mama looked at him, and pointed to the rock. "It looks just like a palm tree."

It did—I had seen illustrations of those trees that Mama said grew along the Carolina coasts—but quite a tiny palm tree. This one stretched up, perfectly centered in the stone, angled to the right, and then a wee bit higher its branches formed, twelve in all, with what appeared to be palm fronds.

Papa did not appear fazed, even when Mama said: "It reminds me of Wilmington, when we'd go visit Aunt Matilda."

"Homesick?" Papa asked.

Mama looked up, her good humor ended. "This is my home, Wil. *Our* home."

Papa bit his lip, and nodded at the hearth. "Put it in the center there."

It would be our showpiece, well, Mama's and mine. We would point it out to visitors, the few we had in those days, and they would smile, admire it, and compliment me on my discovery.

Which I would later learn was just a *crinoid*—Greek for sea lily—a marine animal from thousands of years earlier, and proof that where we now raised cattle had once been covered by an ocean.

Mama knew that ocean bit already: *And it came to pass after seven days, that the waters of the flood were upon the earth.* From Genesis.

I found another fossil, too. Papa remarked that it looked just like a deer heart, and Mama said I should keep it for good luck. That was what I would later discover was a fossilized clam *steinkern*. I still prefer deer heart.

But that was about all of the geology I learned that summer.

Work was hard, but those stones, relatively speaking, were not as heavy as say granite, and Papa, Mama, and I could lay a course of stones in a day. Papa had mixed lump lime, sand, and water, which he had left to form in a pit. When we needed to begin the mortar process, one of us would take some of the lime putty from the pit and mix it with sand—about a one-to-three ratio—which gave us the mortar.

Slowly but surely the house took shape.

The roof had been flat, but Papa decided to

replace it with a pitched roof, bringing in the wood from the thickets. With Uncle Moses and some of Captain Earnhardt's hired men, dropping by every now and then, we even put up a covered porch. There was one door—in time, years after of the time I relate, another would be added to the west, next to the chimney, which would even-tually lead to an addition to the house. We set a long wooden bench—where it came from, I never knew—along the wall on the porch, which was dirt, next to the front door.

No, it was not much of a home, probably more of a bunkhouse, one door and no windows. Papa would add a window, with a heavy shutter, a year later, and a year after that, he put glass in the window. Papa never cared much for the roof. He did that for Mama's sake. Later Uncle Moses would let me know why Papa didn't like the roof. The shingles were wood, and wood would burn. But it never leaked, and the walls were thick and solid, which helped us stay warm in the winter and cool in the summer. During winters, Mama would cook in the fireplace. In the summers, she would cook outside.

The only real concern we had came early in the winter, when our fireplace would be fired up for the first time. That's when the heat would drive out the rattlesnakes that lived under the fireplace.

Home was small, but comfortable. There was a kitchen with a table where we would eat. A living area where we would read and do small chores. Mama and Papa's bedroom was created by a rug that divided the living room from their sleeping quarters, and mine was upstairs in half a loft, which I shared with saddles and tack and supplies until a bunkhouse was later completed.

Our barn looked more like two buildings under one flat, thatched roof. One side was stone, where we would also store food as water flowed from the spring through a trough to keep everything cool. The other part was made of wood, the bottom half of picketed sawed timbers that the sun would eventually warp and dry out, and the upper half built in slats to provide ventilation. We had six stalls, and a tack room. The one door was in the wooden half, and led outside to our corral. To get into the barn, you had to walk through the corral. That made it harder for rustlers or Indians to steal our horses.

We also laid out a fieldstone foundation for a board and batten shop that would be constructed of wood, but for the first year there would be no building, just a forge and anvil and fire pit on the stone floor.

Anyway, that was pretty much my first summer back home. After working sunup to sundown, Mama and I would do our reading from the Bible by the campfire while Papa would tend to the stock and get ready for the next day's work.

Although Moses Gage and Captain Earnhardt

sent a few hands over when he could spare them, it was Mama, Papa, and I that did most of the work until late July, when a man rode up to our place while Mama was cooking breakfast.

He was the one we had seen riding into town when we had first arrived back in Jacksboro. His horse had put on some weight, and the man looked a little filled out himself, wearing a shirt and two boots now, but the same old bib-and-brace overalls.

Papa stood up, adjusting the belted Leech & Rigdon .36-caliber revolver, and waited until the man had reined up.

" 'Mornin'," he said.

Papa nodded.

"Capt'n Earnhardt said you might need a hand."

"Ben's not known for lying," Papa said. "But right now about all I can pay is coffee and biscuits."

He dismounted as if Papa had said $20 a month and found and free rye whiskey.

Mama had already filled a mug of chicory for him, and he took it gratefully, tipping that old Confederate campaign hat, and nodding a casual greeting at me.

"Name's Butler," he said. "Horace Butler."

"Been riding the grubline?" Papa asked.

"Yes, sir. Come home after the war. Only wasn't no home to come back to."

Papa gestured at our unfinished house. "Same here."

Horace Butler sipped the coffee, and thanked Mama profusely when she handed him a plate of biscuits and a little pork from last night's leftovers.

"Settled up in Antelope," he said, dipping a biscuit into the coffee and wolfing it down. Antelope was a small settlement in the northwestern corner of the county, along the West Fork of the Trinity River. I had never been there.

"My pa and me," Horace Butler went on. "Around 'Fifty-Eight. Ma taken me away, though, six months later. Went down to Houston. Joined up with Colonel Terry . . . Big Frank . . . in August of 'Sixty-One. Got paroled at Durham Station, come home, found Mama had been called to Glory in 'Sixty-Three, then come up north to see if I could find my pa."

He stopped to stuff his mouth with the pork, another coffee-dipped biscuit.

Papa waited while he chewed.

Once he swallowed, he added: "He was dead, too. Got drunk. Swallowed his tongue. Leastways, that's what the postmaster up in Antelope told me."

"And your claim?" Papa asked.

Butler drank some coffee, and shook his head as a weary smile stretched across his face. "Pa wasn't much good at Spanish Monte, but he'd bet on it ever' chance he got. Why Ma left him."

A spring wind would still likely blow Horace

Butler away, but he was a man, and a willing worker, I was ten years old, and Mama was a woman. Papa glanced at Mama, and he could tell that she wanted Horace to have a place to bunk for a spell, Mama being given to charitable causes and such. She gave the young man another biscuit, and it, too, vanished immediately. I could tell that Papa was thinking the same thing I was: *He'll eat everything we have.*

But Papa nodded toward Lost Creek, and explained: "Ben Earnhardt's been running my cattle with his. We partner together, but right now this is my job." He motioned toward our progress on the ranch headquarters.

"I done some carpentry work in Houston," Butler said. "Had to do just about everything to help Mama make ends meet." He stood a bit taller as he added: "I was a finishing carpenter."

Papa grinned. Having done some carpentry work in Austin, he must have anticipated the joke.

"I'd get one chore done, and the boss man would tell me . . . 'Well, go and finish this.' And I'd go finish the next chore."

"How are you at masonry?" Papa asked.

"I can learn. Can learn just 'most anything. Had to learn how to be a soldier, a horse soldier, how to ride hard and fight hard." He frowned. "Had to learn how to bury folks, too. Even loaded Big Frank's coffin onto the train after we sent him home from Kentucky in December of 'Sixty-One."

"Well," Papa said, "there are no Yankees here to trouble us."

"Oh, but there is, Mister Braden, they sure is." He had helped himself to the coffee pot on the rock by the fire, and he came up quickly, and pointed toward town.

"Bold as brass, they rode in on the Fourth of July. Set up camp on the southwestern corner of the square. Most of 'em is livin' in tents, but they taken over some buildin's that was vacant. Barkin' orders from the get-go. Sixth Cavalry they is. Colonel Paddy Starr is their leader."

Papa stared at Mama, but neither spoke. The Yankees had arrived in Jacksboro.

Although we had no money to pay him, Horace Butler joined us that morning and would stay on as a hired hand for years. Papa promised him a heifer and a calf, and if we ever drove a herd to Sedalia, he would pay him a real wage, $20 a month and found. He would sleep in the barn, and maybe, if cattle ever became worth something in this part of the country again, they would build a bunkhouse and turn our rawhide outfit into a bona-fide ranch.

So we worked alongside one another, and Horace Butler talked. I learned more about the war from him—or at least his version about riding with Terry's Texas Rangers—over that summer than I ever learned from Papa.

After mustering in at Houston, Colonel Terry had ordered the men to light out for Virginia. Instead, they went to Bowling Green, Kentucky, at the request of General Albert Sidney Johnston. They would be baptized at Woodsonville, Kentucky, where Colonel Benjamin Franklin Terry was killed, and where John Wharton replaced him, briefly. Finally Thomas Harrison was promoted to colonel, and he would lead the regiment for the rest of the war. And what a war.

Shiloh and Murfreesboro in Tennessee. Chickamauga, Chattanooga, and Atlanta. Bentonville, North Carolina, where Horace's horse had been shot out from under him and left him with a broken arm.

"Did you know Burt Pirkle?" I asked.

"Sure," he said that evening, stuffing rabbit into his mouth, and hardly chewing the meat. "He rode with us till the end. You know him?"

"Not really. I went to school with his son . . . in Austin . . . for a short while."

Bobby Ray Pirkle had given me some history of Terry's Texas Rangers, but Horace Butler brought those stories to life.

"Burt was a horse's . . ." He stopped, swallowed, and gave Mama a sheepish grin. "Well, he wasn't much of a soldier."

He wasn't much of a father, either, I thought. *He wasn't much of a man.*

"But most of the boys was top soldiers. Like

163

you, Top Soldier." He grinned. "We sure saw the elephant. Saw some wild times." He picked up his cup to drink some coffee and looked at Papa.

"How 'bout you, Mister Braden?"

"Name's Wil," Papa told him.

"Wil. You saw the elephant, I know."

Papa answered with a shrug, withdrawing into that shell of his.

"Capt'n Earnhardt says you-all was at Sharpsburg."

When Papa's head bobbed, I thought I finally might get to hear those stories I had been making up in my mind, dreaming about, but he said nothing.

"We wasn't at that one, but . . ." Butler whistled and shook his head. "I sure heard some stories."

Papa set his empty cup in the wreck pan. "Time to turn in," he said, and headed for his bedroll.

I frowned, and Mama told me we should read the Bible and practice some arithmetic before it got too dark. We left Horace Butler to finish his supper, leaving the dirty dishes soaking in the water overnight. Horace Butler was no fool. He got Papa's message, and seldom spoke about the war again while around Mama and Papa.

We had one visitor that summer, before school resumed in September. A man and a woman came riding up in a buckboard in the middle of the afternoon. I recognized the man immediately.

"Howdy, Clarke!"

Clarke Earnhardt would have been in his early twenties by then, and he still had that fire in his eyes and that massive chaw of tobacco in his cheek. Narrow hipped and broad shouldered, he set the brake, and leaped out of the buckboard, grinning and spitting juice.

"Pierce Braden," he said, "you best quit growin', else you're gonna be taller than me."

I doubted that. Clarke had to be six-foot-four even without those high-heeled black boots he wore. We shook hands, his massive one devouring mine like the whale swallowing Jonah. He quickly straightened, to sweep off his hat and bow at my mother.

"Missus Martha Jane. It's been far too long."

"Yes it has, Clarke. How's Gretchen?"

"As tolerable as a woman can be livin' with my old man." The tan hat returned to his head, and he hurried to the other side of the buckboard, helping down a thin woman in a red-and-white checked dress and high button boots. The dark-skinned woman wore a blue bonnet. She said nothing, and looked at the ground.

"Pierce, Missus Martha Jane, I'd like you to meet . . ."

Mama was already past him, smiling at the woman—more of a child, she seemed to me, though certainly older than me—and offering her hand.

"Janet," Mama said, "Janet Conley."

Charley's sister. My mouth dropped open.

"Janet Earnhardt, if you please, ma'am," Clarke said, and spit. "For nigh two years."

Janet Conley Earnhardt lifted her head, but did not smile. She bowed and took Mama's hand in her own for just a moment, then dropped it, and looked again at the ground.

"Where's Wil?" Clarke asked.

Mama made a vague gesture. "He and Horace . . . that's the hand Wil has hired . . . rode to the quarry. Probably won't be back until the day's end."

"Sorry we missed him. Place is lookin' fine."

Mama's attention had turned elsewhere. She saw the chests, grips, and furniture in the back of the wagon, secured with ropes and canvas. Even Clarke's stock saddle sat in the back.

"You are . . . ?" Mama could not finish.

Clarke shuffled his feet. "We're gonna try Comanche Springs. On the San Antonio–Chihuahua wagon road. Be better, I think." His head tilted at his bride, and he whispered: "For her." Those bright eyes of his turned sad. "Me, too."

Mama gave him an understanding nod. "Do you know anyone in Comanche Springs?" she asked.

He grinned, but the smile held no joy. "No, ma'am. That's why we're goin' there."

CHAPTER TWELVE

Years would pass before I understood what all of that meant, why Clarke Earnhardt had left Jack County for some place in far West Texas with his wife. Ten-year-olds don't know a whole lot, but in northwestern Texas during those years immediately after the War Between the States, they did grow up fast.

By summer's end, the house and barn were finished. Usually such events called for a fandango or some sort of party, but not at the Braden Ranch. Papa and Horace Butler left to help Ben Earnhardt with the cattle. Mama and I turned the ranch into some semblance of a home.

I did like Horace Butler. He taught me how to throw a lariat, starting with me standing flat-footed and trying to loop the anvil on the stone floor near the barn, until I progressed enough that he decided I should start roping from the saddle on his bay mare.

He taught me how to read sign, although I guess Uncle Moses would have made a better teacher, for sometimes I'd point out a track, ask Horace what it was, and he'd answer: "Some animal."

Once, when he was working the forge, he pulled out the iron he had fashioned, per Papa's orders, and let me slap the brand on a red cedar plank. When I pulled away the hot iron, I looked at the blackened imprint the brand had made.

"The Rafter B," Horace told me. "We'll be slappin' that mark on beeves and horses from now on."

He let me nail the plank over the barn door. As a finishing carpenter, he even gave me advice. "Hold your mouth right. That way you'll hit the real nail instead of a fingernail."

"How do I hold my mouth right?" I asked.

"That's the secret every carpenter's gotta learn."

After one bruised thumb that temporarily relieved me of a fingernail, I learned that secret, too. Mine was by pressing my top lip over my bottom lip. Say what you may, but I've never hit the wrong type of nail since.

Mostly, however, when we were alone, Horace Butler told me about the war, the battles he had fought in. Papa usually wasn't home for supper, instead drifting home well after the moon had risen, worn out from riding the ranges, to eat cold biscuits and beans. Mama would be getting things set up for breakfast, and I'd be alone with Horace Butler, listening. . . .

"We was supposed to have gone to Virginy, like your pa went with Hood's boys," Horace once said. "We was also supposed to be horse soldiers . . . cavalry, but right before we left, by boat, for New Orleans, the colonel told us to send our horses home. Boat didn't even sail all the way to New Orleans. We had to walk about half that distance. Which irritated us. Seems they desired our presence in Kentucky, so we turned north. Lost one poor boy . . . disremember his name . . . to measles in Nashville, then made it to Bowling Green. They said we'd be the Eighth Texas Calvary, but we told them boys . . . 'No, sir. By grab, we're Terry's Texas Rangers.'

"Best thing about it was that we got us some fine mounts in Kentucky. Nothin' like them ol' nags we'd had out here. Bunch of generals and the likes wanted us to have sabers, but we told 'em . . . 'No, sir, we'll keep our Bowie knifes, by grab.'"

"Did you buy the horses?" I asked.

He sipped his coffee. "Let's just say we . . . u-m-m-m . . . acquired 'em."

More and more soldiers died in Kentucky, but not from battle wounds. Mcasles, dysentery, camp fever. Half of the time during that first winter, more than half of the Rangers were sick in hospitals. By the end of the year, more than eighty had died.

Oh, Horace and his fellow soldiers saw some battles. They saw the elephant at Woodsonville, where Colonel Terry was killed, firing shotguns from horseback into the "scared Huns" of the 32nd Indiana. After Fort Henry and Fort Donelson fell, they retreated with the other Confederate outfits to Corinth, Mississippi. Then came Shiloh, and those bloody two days along the banks of the Tennessee River.

"We was with Colonel Nathan Bedford 'By Thunder' Forrest, and he was leadin' us, not our ol' 'Jimtown' major who was yellow as they come and should've been hung in Kentucky. Yanks was tryin' to strike our rear, so Forrest, he gets us to ride with a few of his Third Tennessee boys, and we go chargin' through a bunch of felled trees.

"Ol' Forrest, he says . . . 'Forward!' And that's about all we needed to hear. We charged. Yes, we charged. Left 'em Tennessee boys tryin' to keep their mounts from runnin' after us.

"We don't stop till we's ten, twenty paces from the bluebellies, and can see their bayonets a-gleamin' in the sun. Pig-stickers? Ag'in' Terry's Texas Rangers with double-barrel shotguns. Boy, that was glory, some glory. Blood and thunder. My gun had twenty buckshot in each barrel, and we fired into them bluecoats. Yanks went down like they was a covey of quail. 'Em boys who wasn't dead or dyin' or blown to bits skedaddled, but we wasn't lettin' 'em get back to their mammies. No, sir. We slung our shotguns, drawed our pistols, and lit after 'em.

"Taken some prisoners, but most we jus' left dead or dyin' till some of 'em reached the blue-belly line. That's when we decided to head back, see if those Third Tennessee boys was still tryin' to hold their horses still."

Horace Butler shook his head, eyes gleaming. "I still ain't quite figured out how we lost that battle. Or the blasted war."

He would tell other stories, of Perryville and Murfreesboro, Chickamauga, and bedeviling Sherman's troops as they burned their way across Georgia. The one I remember most is his account of Shiloh in April of '62. Anyway, that was the story I reimagined when I rode Nutmeg across Jack County. In those stories, of course, I was riding with Hood's Texas Brigade—forgetting that the 1st Texas was infantry—and galloping to glory alongside my father and Uncle Jake.

Who's Nutmeg, you ask?

She was a light brown mare with four white feet and a white nose. Papa bought her, or traded for her, and Uncle Moses gentled her, and brought her to the ranch in the latter part of August.

I had always hoped that Papa might buy Linda Ferdig Riley Lasater from Moses Gage, until I learned that the dun mare had been stolen from Uncle Moses. Often, I wondered if that Kiowa boy who had traded me the knife was the horse thief.

"You dead certain this is the hoss you want?" Moses Gage asked Papa when he rode up, leading the brown behind him.

Papa nodded, and Mama put her hands on my shoulder. I held my breath.

Shaking his head, Uncle Moses said: "One white foot, buy 'em. Two white feet, try 'em. Three white feet, careful with 'em. Four white feet and white on his nose, bash in his brains and feed 'em to the crows."

Mama said: "One white foot, send her far away. Two white feet, try her for one day. Three white feet, sell her to a friend. Four white feet, keep her till the end."

Uncle Moses chuckled, and swung down from his big black. "Your funeral, I reckon." Ground-reining his horse, he led the brown toward the porch, and then presented the reins to me.

I looked first at Mama, who beamed down at me, and then over at Papa.

"She's your responsibility," Papa said. "Birthday present."

"It . . . it's not my . . . birthday," I said.

"Reckon I missed plenty," Papa said. "Take 'er. But I'm siding with Moses. Never cared much for a horse with four white feet."

The stirrups were too high, and lowering stirrups meant undoing a lot of laces, so Uncle Moses boosted me into the saddle, which was too big.

"He'll grow into it," Papa assured everyone.

"What's her name?" I asked.

Uncle Moses snorted. "I'd call 'er Glue Bait." He winked, to let me know he had been joking.

I said: "I'll call her Nutmeg." I have no idea

why that name popped into my head, but her ears flickered at the name, and I laughed. "She likes it!"

I rode to the corral, keeping Nutmeg at a walk, then back to the porch.

"Ain't what I'd call a ride," Uncle Moses said.

Mama tilted her head toward the flats. "Here comes Horace," she said. "Why don't you ride out to meet him?"

First I wet my lips. Then I pulled down the brim of my hat. Finally I neck-reined Nutmeg, and kicked her sides. We started out at a walk, before I eased into a smooth trot. Of all the horses I've owned, Nutmeg remains the one that wouldn't break my spine when trotting. Even Linda Ferdig Riley Lasater's gait had been anything but comfortable. At last we moved into a lope, and she smoothly kicked into a gallop.

I did not picture myself as some Civil War soldier, leading a glorious charge. But I felt the wind in my face, felt the power of a good horse underneath me, and saw the prickly pear, the stones, and the faraway Texas horizon, racing past me in a blur. Horace Butler had reined in his mare, and he watched, grinning, as I circled around him, slowing my new horse into a walk, and then stopping beside him. Our meeting was brief.

"Howdy!" I said.

"Race you!" Spurring the bay, Horace Butler

bolted toward the Rafter B headquarters. Nutmeg did not wait for my response. She tore up the ground catching up.

I won. Well, Horace Butler let me win. Of that I am certain. All these years later, and yet everything about that early evening remains chiseled into my memories.

Mama, in her dress of brown poplin, which she had made herself from a bolt of fabric she had bought in Jacksboro. Her eyes, filled with tears of joy. The way she looked at Papa, and how she moved closer to him, took his big hand in her own, and how their fingers locked.

Uncle Moses, shaking his head while biting off a mouthful from the twist of tobacco, repeating his superstitions and dislike for horses with four white feet but saying that I might change his thinking.

Horace Butler, trying to catch his breath, allowing how if I had been riding with Terry's Texas Rangers during the late unpleasantness, bluecoats wouldn't be commanding much of Jacksboro.

And Nutmeg, munching on the carrots Mama had brought out of the house and given me to feed my horse. Uncle Moses reckoned that she must be part Morgan, half Pegasus. I knew she was nothing but a mustang, fourteen hands—if that—hard legged, short backed, narrow chested. Her almond-shaped eyes were green. Most horses of

174

her breed had brown eyes, although some bald-faced ones I'd seen had blue eyes.

"Spanish blood in her," Uncle Moses said. "Her grandma's grandma's grandma might've come over with Coronado."

Clear as yesterday, I remember, as I started to lead Nutmeg to the corral to unsaddle her, rub her down, and grain her, Papa saying: "Horse like that'll come in handy."

And Mama's response: "And save me a lot of worry and time. School starts next week."

Since I had Nutmeg, I did not mind school so much. Nancy Livermore could no longer say I didn't ride my own horse, and I bet Charley Conley would have been envious of my mustang mare—had he not quit school.

I was not the only child who rode to school. We would unsaddle our mounts and turn them loose in a round pen, bring our books and lunch pails inside, and try to learn something. Well, some of us, anyway.

Riding to school was fun. I would make up my own adventures, especially when I rode into the woods of oaks and pecans, Chickasaw plums and wild mustang grapes. It seemed like Sherwood Forrest compared to the clumps of mesquite that sprouted up here and there at the Rafter B headquarters.

But an even better time came when we went

outside to play after lunch, because sometimes Bobby Weatherly, Jim Fountain, and I—and even, on occasion, Nancy Livermore—would walk to town to watch the Yankees.

They had taken over the center of town. Built picket houses, made by setting logs on end, chinking the cracks with wood chips and mud, and using lashed poles covered with dirt as roofing. Crates had been turned into doors. Only the fireplaces looked permanent. Five companies from the 6th Cavalry had turned the center of Jacksboro into a fort, each company sharing six of those . . . well, I wouldn't call them homes.

"Look at 'em," Bobby Weatherly whispered. "Hard to see how we lost to the likes of 'em."

A bluecoat barked some orders, and a bunch of troopers swung into their saddles. The officer yelled something more, motioned with his gauntleted hand, and they rode away from the community of rawhide. They rode toward us, the hoofs of their horses making sucking sounds as they trudged through eight inches of thick, gooey mud. Some Jacksboro citizens came out of their stores on Rat Row to watch, smoking cigars.

"Look at them Yanks," one man said with a chuckle. "They already look horse whipped."

For certain, they didn't look excited. Even the officer seemed reluctant to lead this mission. Most of them sat slouched in those back-breaking things they called saddles, beard stubble and dirt on their faces and clothes, their boots and stirrups already caked with that Jack County mud.

"Let 'em be," another voice said. "They's here to protect us."

The first man shook his head and spit with contempt.

Another said: "They ain't gonna catch no Injuns, not on them mounts."

We kids just watched, their gear clinking, even their horses looking tired. That last man had been quite right. The horses the 6th Cavalry rode seemed half starved, already sweating and lethargic, as if they were suffering from colic. Which they probably were.

"At least they're goin' after Injuns now," said one of the men, "and not tormentin' us citizens with all that Reconstruction business."

When we mentioned this to Miss Riley back at school, she told us to put away our Readers. Being a Yankee from Rhode Island, she had her prejudices and biases, and none of us seemed surprised when she defended the 6th Cavalry.

"They are far from home," she reminded us, "and with an ugly job to do. Put yourself in their shoes."

"Oooohhh," Julie Jamison said. "I wouldn't want to put my stockings inside those nasty things!"

We laughed. Miss Riley frowned.

"They are two hundred miles from the railroad," she said. "I don't know how far away the nearest Army fort is. They are seventy miles from the Indian Territory. Hundreds and hundreds of miles from their loved ones, their homes. And they are here to protect you, your mothers, your fathers, your sisters and brothers. And what thanks do we give them?"

"Well, one fellow spit at 'em bluebellies," Bobby Weatherly said.

Again, we laughed, and, once more, Miss Riley did not.

Soon we would see cavalry patrols passing by the school on a regular basis. No longer did we have to run to town to see the Yanks.

On the afternoon of Wednesday, October 24th, I learned why.

The mail coach ran twice a week, on good weeks, between Waco and Fort Smith. Every now and then when I was riding to or from school, I would see the coach and, while shielding my eyes from the dust, wave at the men atop.

This time, I saw the mud wagon, but it was not raising dust or churning up mud. It lay on its side. There were no mules. Just dead people. They were the first corpses I'd ever seen, and they were not pretty.

The driver lay near the overturned wagon,

arrows pinning him to the ground. Unlike Hog Clagett, he had not survived his scalping. The messenger had been propped up against an oak, three arrows in his chest, and a grisly wound in his forehead, blackened by powder from a close-range shot. The Indians had not scalped him. Perhaps they had respected him as a warrior.

They had not had respect for the third man, who I learned later was the Army paymaster. Usually the coach carried only mail, but for some reason the paymaster had been on this run. He had been tied to the rear wagon wheel, and the Indians had dug a pit, which they had filled with the chopped spokes of the front wheel and other brush and tinder and then set afire.

This had happened well beyond Jacksboro, so I kicked Nutmeg into a lope, and raced for home. More scared than I had ever been by the time I'd arrived, Mama had to pull me out of the saddle, envelope me with her arms, and scream for Papa, who ran from the barn.

"They're dead!" I wailed. "They're all dead!"

"Who's dead?" Mama asked.

Although I could barely get out the words, something I said registered with Papa, who tossed down his hammer, and yelled at Horace Butler: "Ride to Capt'n Earnhardt's!"

Papa was already swinging up onto Nutmeg's back. "Inside," he told Mama.

He wore his belted pistol, for the full moon had peaked the previous evening. I couldn't see him as he rode away on my mare. I feared I might never see him again.

Captain Earnhardt, Hog Clagett, Moses Gage, and others were at our home before Papa had returned. By then, I had calmed down some. Papa sent Nutmeg with one of the captain's men to the corral, and asked the cowhand to saddle his big gelding. Mama was already busy frying corndodgers and brewing coffee, and filling a grain bag with the hot bread.

"Mail coach," Papa said. "Three men dead. Mules stolen. Don't know what else."

"Where?" Captain Earnhardt demanded.

Papa made a vague gesture. "Seven, eight miles from town."

"That's a sight close to . . . ," Ellis Morrell did not finish the statement, and looked apologetically at my father. It was much, much too close to our home.

"Sign?" Captain Earnhardt asked.

Papa made another gesture.

Captain Earnhardt cursed. "Well, maybe those Kiowa savages'll be slow in gettin' 'cross the Red."

"Comanche," Papa corrected. "At least the arrows were Comanche."

Captain Earnhardt made a vile reference about

all Indians, and didn't bother to apologize for using such language in front of my mother and me.

"Full moon'll give us a chance to trail 'em," Captain Earnhardt said.

"You don't want to fetch the soldiers from Jacksboro?" Horace Butler asked.

"No, by Jacks. Why would I do that? Blue-coats'd just slow us down, and I ain't takin' no orders from no bluebelly. We'll do this ourselves. Way we Texans have done if for a thousand years."

His math was off, but everyone understood his point. The men filed out of our home, and Mama held my hand as she stood in the doorway.

"You stay here," Papa told Horace Butler, and then, his eyes settling on Hog Clagett, added: "You, too, Hog."

Clagett whipped off that big black hat of his, revealing his scalped head, and you could tell he wanted to protest. After all, this was his chance at revenge, but something in Papa's eyes told Clagett that he would brook no argument, and the hat returned to cover his damaged head. "All right, Wil. Be careful."

Papa swung into the saddle. Uncle Moses tossed Papa the big Enfield. After shifting the long gun into his right hand, Papa accepted the sack of corndodgers in his left, which he wrapped around the saddle horn.

"He's done with school," Papa told Mama. "Understand?"

Mama nodded. And Captain Earnhardt, Papa, and the rest of those men galloped into the fading light.

CHAPTER THIRTEEN

After that, my schooling became Mama's responsibility. We had our Readers, and our Bible, and I, of course, kept poring through Dana's *Text-Book of Geology*, though Mama would have me reading Tennyson more than she would let me learn about rock formations and Paleozoic and Mesozoic and Cenozoic times.

Yet most of my education would come from Horace Butler and Uncle Moses, and, on rare occasion, even from Papa. Mama taught me in the evenings, and maybe for an hour on Sundays after we had read the Bible together and prayed. The rest of the time, I learned . . . by hard work.

I saddled Nutmeg. I groomed her, picked the sharp rocks and packed dirt out of her iron shoes. I worked on the buildings, in the corrals, in the garden. I learned to rope, and how to sit in a saddle, how to tighten the cinch. I even figured out how to keep my seat—sometimes—when Nutmeg started feeling frisky in the mornings, and would buck two or more jumps before settling down.

I also tried to teach myself a few things. Riding along a creekbed, I might dismount, pretending to check the saddle, or just to let Nutmeg drink. In reality, I would turn over rocks, study them, classify what they were, while always hunting for fossils, and hoping to unearth a dinosaur bone or two.

I did find a few fossils, and, once, a snake when I stupidly turned over a stone. I heard it sing out like a rattlesnake. Tumbling back, I let an oath slip off my tongue and wished like blazes that Papa would have let me carry a revolver so I could have blown the snake's head off. Actually I likely would have shot my own foot. Nutmeg jerked back, and the snake stopped play acting. Once I had caught my breath and my heart had settled back into its natural beat, I rose to dust myself off, and walked back to my horse, saying to Nutmeg: "Bull snake. It's just a bull snake, girl." Which it was. Bull snakes look a lot like rattlesnakes, and even can imitate them, but they are not venomous.

I swung into Nutmeg's saddle, but I forgot that snakes—even bull snakes—make horses skittish, and she did more than two jumps that time. She did six, probably more, but after six I went sailing over her head and into the creek, skinning my right arm, and ripping my sleeve on the rocks. The reins also burned my right hand, and that leather cut hurt worse than the raw forearm and the humiliation. However, I held tight to the rein, which prevented me from further embarrassment. I was not left afoot.

Coming up to my knees, I managed to grip the other dangling rein and held Nutmeg until she calmed down. After that, I checked the saddle straps, washed my raw hand and bleeding arm in the creek, and mounted the horse again.

That's the rule of the cowboy, I had been told time and again. If you get bucked off, get right back on.

I rode off, away from any fossils, away from the bull snake, and went back to work, hoping that the sun would dry my clothes before anyone saw me. Ripped shirt sleeves and wounds could be explained easy enough. Working cattle was dangerous. I could have torn my shirt on the briars and brambles that grew along the water paths. I did not have to admit that Nutmeg had bucked me off, because she had not.

How could that be? Well, that's another rule I learned, this one from Uncle Moses. "If nobody saw the horse wreck," he told me, "it didn't happen."

That is not to say that I escaped detection from everyone.

When I reached home late that afternoon, Mama washed my arm, and put some sort of medicine on it that burned like blazes. She also dabbed the rein burn with butter and another ointment, but that did not hurt so much. When Papa came home, she told him that I needed a pair of gloves if I would be working cattle.

That brought Papa to inspect my hand. "What happened, Top Soldier?" he asked.

"Rein burn," I said.

He looked at my bandaged arm. And the rips in the knees of my duck trousers that I had not noticed until then. "When you get to Goldman's," Papa told Mama, "you might get him a pair of leggings, too. Have Ezra put the chaps and gloves on our bill."

Those I know here in Leechburg today, decades since the events I relate, do not believe me when I tell them that I never had any desire to become a cowboy. Oh, I did it—some might even say I did it well for a mere boy—but it never found a place in my heart, which is why I work underground now, with dim light, inspecting and moving and sometimes even collecting rocks.

Many of my friends have read and believed Mr. Wister's romantic image that he painted all too well in *The Virginian* last year, but I found nothing romantic about spending twelve to sixteen hours on the back of a horse, or slapping that Rafter B brand on the hides of calves, until the smell of burning hide embedded itself in my clothes, my hair, my nostrils.

The sun baked you. The wind blasted you.

Dust choked you, or blinded you, or did both.

Throughout the rest of 1867, I worked for Papa, but naturally collected no wages, and I rarely saw the friends, or enemies, I had made at Miss Linda Riley's school because no one came to visit us, and school was in my past. Therefore, no one could see me in my gloves and chaps and hat. They could not see how hard my hands had become, or how the muscles had hardened on my body, or how the sun and wind had bronzed my face. I grew, too.

"Boy's shootin' up like a weed," Captain Earnhardt would say on his visits. "Make a top hand, Wil." Then he would stop speaking, and begin cursing his own son, who had moved away to Comanche Springs with his new wife.

Papa might even smile, or ride his horse up to me and measure how high I sat in the saddle. It depended on his mood. Usually, though, he would nod, and I knew it was time for me to ride back to find more cattle, or stoke the fire we had built for branding, or lead my horse to the pen, or help Solomon Burke wash the dirty dishes in the wreck pan.

All this work, all the branding and the sweating, all the headaches and cuts, bruises and chaffed flesh, and it was in the spring of 1868, when I was twelve years old, that Papa broke my heart.

You recall that I wrote about how we came up from Austin after the War Between the States, and that we had followed what would become the Great Texas Cattle Trail. By 1868, it was just that.

Before Texas drovers used what is known in history books—for this era actually did not last many years—as the Chisholm Trail, they herded beef north by way of the Shawnee Trail to Sedalia, Missouri, or Baxter Springs, Kansas. That's where Captain Earnhardt and Papa planned on taking their cattle to market, because in those days beef was not worth a nickel in Texas.

The war had given Yankees a taste for beef, and Texas had plenty of longhorns, most of them wild and mean and living off the land for years. Late during the war, I heard it said, a man named Jesse Chisholm—some part-Scot, part-Cherokee trader in the Indian Territory—began hauling trade goods to various Indian villages from his trading post along the Arkansas River in Kansas. He went south, of course, into the Indian Territory, and in 1867 the cowboys riding herd on O.W. Wheeler's twenty-four hundred longhorns saw the wagon tracks at the North Canadian River.

Wheeler, with a few partners, had bought his beeves in San Antonio, and was trying to avoid the troubles other drovers had found in Missouri with border gangs and farmers who did not like cattle trampling their crops, or killing their own milch cows with what Missourians and later Kansans called "Texas Fever." The state of Missouri had even put up a quarantine line, prohibiting Texas herds, and the market at Baxter Springs never proved all that profitable.

Abilene, Kansas, however, wanted Texas cattle, thanks to a smart Yankee from Illinois named Joseph G. McCoy. McCoy talked the officials who bossed the Kansas Pacific into laying a siding in Abilene, which was home to a few merchants and farmers back then. McCoy built holding pens and loading chutes, and told Texas ranchers and drovers that Abilene was their future.

Wheeler was the first to come up north, but he didn't even know about Abilene or Joseph McCoy until his crew found Jesse Chisholm's wagon tracks. His plan was to winter the cattle on the Kansas plains, and then trail the herd to sell in California. He brought word back, though, and so did McCoy, who was a businessman out for profit. Wheeler was far from the last, of course. I heard that Abilene shipped out thirty-five thousand head of longhorns to the packing houses during that spring.

The Chisholm Trail—a name that I did not hear until maybe 1870 or perhaps even a few years later—had been born. In 1868, Papa and Captain Earnhardt decided to make a drive.

Forgetting all about those stories I had longed to hear from Papa about the war, I grew fascinated with the idea of heading up the trail, and seeing something beyond Texas. Besides, my readings and interests had educated me on a few things about Kansas. Earlier that year, some Yankee saw-bones at Fort Wallace had discovered an almost complete skeleton of a Plesiosaur. Fossilized plants had been discovered years earlier in Ellsworth County, and someone had even found shark teeth somewhere in the state.

"Shark teeth!" I remembered exclaiming to Mama. "In Kansas!"

" 'And the rain was upon the earth forty days and forty nights,' " Mama reminded me, and waited.

That one was easy. "Genesis," I told her.

I did not know if Abilene lay in Ellsworth County (it did not) or was near Fort Wallace (not even close) or exactly where the shark teeth had been found (I still don't know today), but I thought if I could get to Kansas, I might find some really interesting rocks or dinosaur bones. The way to do that, I figured, was to show Papa and Captain Earnhardt just how good of a cowboy I had become.

All it did was almost cost me a finger.

Finding some old mossyhorn stuck in a bog by the creek—the winter and spring had been wet that year—I resolved to pull the stubborn steer out myself. I tossed a loop over its wide horns, for I had become a fair hand with a lariat, and, after dallying the rope around the horn, I spurred Nutmeg and headed up the slope away from the bog and longhorn.

Cattle are stupid. The steer fought, even though

I yelled to him that I was trying to save his sorry hide, although I used a few other choice words and phrases since Mama remained out of earshot. I had picked up quite the vocabulary in a year or two of working alongside men who could not speak a complete sentence without including profanity.

Nutmeg stumbled on the slope, and she twisted, whinnying, and went down the bank in a cloud of dust and rolling rocks. I kept my seat, even when the mare fell onto her front legs. Thinking she might roll, I kicked free of the stirrups, but my great horse righted herself, snorting and turning. I stopped the turn with a hard pull of the reins, and, once she had settled, I reached over to pat her neck.

"You all right, girl?" I asked.

The steer, still wedged in the mud, bawled. I leaped out of the saddle, and checked Nutmeg's legs. Horses are tough, and she seemed fine, so I remounted, and summoned even more determination to get that longhorn out of the mud.

Once I had loosened the dally, I rode back, trying to find an easier way up the hill. Straight ahead, however, seemed the best option, so when I got in position, I attempted the dally again. What I mean, of course, is that I wanted to wrap the end of my lariat around the saddle horn two or three times, to make it secure, so Nutmeg would do most of the work. She was strong, and I did not think the longhorn could be held that fast in the creek's bank.

He wasn't. As I tried the dally, the longhorn jerked up, and managed to pull his front legs from the mire. That movement pulled the lariat, and my pointer finger got caught between the rope and the horn.

Falling out of the saddle, I crashed onto the rocks. Nutmeg stumbled, and fell again, this time rolling over on her side three or four times. Thankfully I had gone down the other way, but I came up clutching my hand, screaming louder than a chicken being pursued by a fox.

Sound carries a long way in that country, and, within five minutes, Horace Butler and Ellis Morrell were galloping toward me. They leaped from their geldings before even coming to a stop, and their spurs jingled as they covered the last few feet down the bank of the creek.

"Top Soldier!" Morrell shouted. "What is it?"

"Where you hurt?" Horace Butler asked.

Doubled over on my knees, I clutched my right hand as tight as I could, blood seeping through leather fingers of the glove. Any answer I gave, however, had to have been nonsensical. Pain was searing through my hand and arm.

I even fought Ellis Morrell as he tried to loosen my hand to have a look as I held it tight against my chest. I mean I fought hard. I feared if I let go of my hand, it might come off at my wrist.

"Grab his shoulders," Morrell told Horace, who did.

Only then did Morrell manage to pull my hand away. He gently pulled off the glove. Like a razor-sharp knife, the lariat had cut through the glove's deerskin finger.

"It's cut deep . . . ," he said. Even though I was yelling, I heard him clearly.

"Get that steer out of the mud," Morrell barked as he eased me to my feet. Because, Morrell knew, cattle came first.

"Then light a shuck and find Wil. I'll fetch Top Soldier here to Missus Braden." He had already loosened his bandanna and was wrapping it around my finger.

CHAPTER FOURTEEN

Folks who knew her often said that my mother should have been a nurse. Or even a doctor. They didn't know any better. Mama *was* a nurse. *And* a doctor. Because she was the wife of a rancher in Jack County, Texas, she had grown accustomed to doctoring.

Over the years, she had stitched up plenty of cuts. She had come up with an ointment of her own concoction to treat bad sunburns. Many a time she had wrapped a prickly pear poultice over a boil. Three-quarters of a teaspoon of powder pectin dissolved in a glass of wild berry juice, drunk once a day, would ease a cowhand's arthritis. Bicarbonate of potassa with a lemon juice chaser would treat rheumatism. She worked on horses, too, when they came up lame or caught the colic or were cut from falls or briars or cinches pulled too tight.

"Missus Braden! Missus Braden!" Ellis Morrell was yelling as he rode up toward the house. He had not slowed down his blue roan gelding since he had pulled me up in front of him, his left arm wrapped tightly around my chest.

I saw Mama rush out of the house as Morrell covered the last few yards at a lope, then jerked the roan to a hard stop. Mama ran to me as Morrell and I came out of the saddle.

"What happened?" Mama asked as she quickly removed her apron and tossed it onto the ground.

"Lariat, ma'am," Morrell said. "Got a deep gash in his pointer finger when he was tryin' to get a dumb steer out of the mud."

I had dropped to my knees, and only then was Mama able to pull my hand away from my chest and begin to unwrap Morrell's makeshift bandage.

Mama sucked in a breath when she saw my finger.

She helped me up, replaced Morrell's bandage, and guided me to the bench on our front porch. "Hold it tight, Pierce," she said. "You're going to be fine."

She lifted it, and placed it on my chest above

my heart. I could smell the blood, and it almost made me sick. "I'll be right back. You'll be fine."

I heard the door open and bang shut.

"There's a bottle of brandy on the table, Ellis," Mama told Morrell when she came back outside, carrying her medicine kit and some water. "Bring it out and then get two chairs and set them out in the sun so I can see what I'm doing."

"Yes'm." His spurs chimed.

Mama said: "Ellis?"

"Yes'm?"

"Don't drink the brandy."

"Yes'm."

I sat on the bench. The chairs were soon sitting in the yard where the sun would give Mama plenty of light. She came to me and grabbed me by the arms, squeezing them hard but keeping her voice gentle.

"Pierce, I need you to stand up."

I hesitated.

"Stand up!"

When I did, dizziness almost dropped me to the flagstone floor of the porch. Mama guided me out into the sun and eased me into one of the chairs.

About that time, Papa and Horace Butler were galloping into the yard. Mama turned her back to them, bringing my finger close to her bosom to protect it from the dust.

"Pierce!" Papa yelled. He did not call me Top Soldier.

The dust settled, and Mama turned back, saying to Papa: "Hold his right arm, Wil. Hold it tight against the arm of the chair."

I could not recall my mother ever having ordered Papa to do anything. Usually she'd just mention that it was time for him to do something, like take a bath. This time, she had turned into General John Bell Hood, or maybe even Robert E. Lee.

Papa obeyed, grimacing when he saw my finger.

"Horace," Mama said, "you hold his left arm. Hold it tight. Ellis, I need you to get down here. . . . Make sure he doesn't kick. Closer. Press tight. That's good."

Mama put a wooden stick in my mouth. "Bite down," she said.

I obeyed.

"This is going to hurt, Pierce. It's going to hurt more than you've ever hurt," she explained to me calmly, adding: "I'm sorry." Then she poured the brandy over my finger.

Fiery pain crawled from my hand and up my arm. I shrieked, and fought the hands pinning my arms to the chair. I tried to kick out, but Ellis Morrell stopped that with his chest and body. Dizziness almost caused me to faint, which is likely what Mama hoped would happen, yet I remained conscious.

Mama prayed as she held the skin of my finger

together and began to sew my finger together with the threaded horse hair.

That is when, mercifully, I passed out.

For several days I stayed at home, my finger wrapped in a whiskey-soaked bandage except when Mama removed it to examine her handi-work. She always made me close my eyes when she did this, which I did not take as a promising sign. I had heard of gangrene, and dreaded smelling some kind of rot as the bandages were removed, but the only scents that reached my nostrils were coffee and bacon and lemon cookies.

I ate a lot of lemon cookies—the one good thing about being invalided out of cowboy duty.

I stare at my finger now, all these years later. Yes, it's a little bent, and the scar shows. It bends, though, and doesn't hurt. It works, for which I owe my mother.

At the time, it remained swollen, but Mama said I would be fine, and that I should stay away from lariats until the scabs had fallen away, and she had removed the stitches.

Mama was making black-eyed peas and corn-bread for supper, and I was sitting, flexing my finger when there occurred a ruction in the yard. We looked at each other and stepped outside into the sun.

Horace Butler was driving a covered wagon into

our yard, pulled by a team of four mules, with Papa and Captain Earnhardt riding on either side of the wagon.

"Martha," Captain Earnhardt called out, "you gotta see what kind of conveyance Wil here come up with!"

Reining in the dapple, Papa swung from the saddle and shook his head. "It's not my invention."

"Balderdash," Earnhardt said, as he rode to the rear of the wagon, and, without leaving his saddle, began fiddling with something. At this Horace Butler set the brake, leaped from the box, and hurried to the back of the wagon, yelling: "Don't break it, Capt'n! Don't break it 'fore we've headed up the trail!"

Mama and I glanced at one another, and then walked to the wagon.

The tailgate was open, braced up by a two-by-four on a hinge that propped it up, creating a long table. It had been fastened to a box filled with drawers, cabinets, and shelves. Secured on one side hung a coffee mill, while a lantern swayed back and forth from a cast-iron bar at the top of the box. Between the two wheels on the left side, a water barrel had been secured, and along either side of the barrel hung ropes, hammer, axe, cleaver, and wrench. Underneath the wagon bed a cowhide had been secured to the corners, and when I kneeled down, I discovered it carried wood and dried buffalo dun. Up front was a jockey box, filled with other tools. The shelves, cabinets, and drawers were empty, except for one big coffee pot, and when I climbed up on the wheel, to look inside, all I found were a couple of bedrolls in the back next to the box.

I jumped down and returned to Mama's side.

"It's a chuckwagon," Captain Earnhardt said. "For the trail to Abilene."

"I do declare." This kitchen on wheels amazed Mama, and it was almost better outfitted than our own.

"Wil's idea," Earnhardt bragged.

"No," Papa said. "Got it from Charley Goodnight."

With his partner, Oliver Story, Goodnight had driven a cattle herd from Fort Belknap to the reservation at Bosque Redondo near Fort Sumner, New Mexico Territory, back in 1866. He had converted an old Studebaker into what he called the chuckwagon, and they would become staples on cattle drives over the years. Papa had merely remembered what he had seen in Fort Belknap and what Goodnight had told him.

"Who's your cook?" Mama asked.

"Solomon Burke," Papa answered.

"Can't cook worth a hoot and a holler," Captain Earnhardt said, "but he can drive a team of mules and handle a spade."

I looked at the chuck box, and saw the Rafter B burned into one side. Right beside it was Captain

198

Earnhardt's brand, the Circle E. They were partners again. Well, I guess they had always been.

I could not contain my excitement. "When do we leave?" I asked.

"Two days," Captain Earnhardt sang out, and Papa frowned.

"Horace," Papa said, "fetch that spare axle from the shed. Martha, can you show Ben those sacks of flour and beans? We'll have need of them when we light out for Abilene."

They walked away to their chores, and Papa gave me that hard stare that broke my heart before he even spoke the words.

"Top Soldier," he said, "I need you to stay close to your ma this time."

"I'm a good cowboy, Papa," I said. I held out my hand, and bent my pointer finger, which caused me to cringe because it hurt. Maybe I had worked it too much that day.

He pretended he had not seen the pain in my face and he came up to me and put his hand on my shoulder. "I know that." He paused before adding: "Don't know what to expect on this drive, Top Soldier," he said at last. "It's better than four hundred miles, we think, through Indian Territory, and, wet as it's been down here, we figure the Red River, the Canadian, and the Arkansas will be hard crossing. Creeks and streams will be tough, too. I'd rest easier if you were here, looking after you mother."

"I'm thirteen years old," I told him, but had to add: "practically."

"In a year," he said. "You're twelve now." He sighed. "There will be other drives. Now, go help your mother. I'll give Horace a hand with that axle."

It took them seven weeks to reach Abilene, and not quite three to return home. A long time, certainly, but we were lucky in that we lived in North Texas. Those from that wild cow country south of San Antonio and north of Corpus Christi had to endure much longer drives to the railhead in Kansas.

The day after they left, Uncle Moses rode to our house, with a war bag full of his gear and a mule deer strapped behind his cantle.

"Can't eat all this meat by myself," he announced to Mama.

"You two butcher it," she said, "and I'll cook it."

So I grabbed some knives and a cleaver, and followed Moses Gage to the place where we cleaned our meat near the creek.

He gutted the deer, tossing the entrails into the water. "Make the catfish happy," he said. "You been fishin' yet, Top Soldier?"

My head shook.

"Ever et catfish?"

My head bobbed.

"You liked it when you did et it?"

I shrugged.

"Well, maybe me and you'll go fishin' tomorrow. That sound fine to you?"

Again I shrugged.

"Ain't much for talk, is you, Top Soldier? You ain't found no dinosaur bones or nothin'?"

My head shook.

He sighed. "How's your finger?"

With a shrug, I showed him.

"Your mama's a wonder. I come down with the gout two weeks back. Should come see her, I reckon."

Another shrug.

"I do somethin' to rile you, Top Soldier?"

I stopped looking at my boots and shook my head.

He washed his hands in the creek, and, with his back to me, he said: "You know, Master Pierce, they didn't invite me to go on that cattle drive, neither."

Of course, he stayed with us for the more than two months that Papa and the others were gone, and not to eat all of the venison or to show me how to catch and clean a catfish, of which we caught plenty. Mama fried them up for both supper and breakfast.

This was through May and into June, and when the full moon rose, we found ourselves welcoming another visitor, which caused my hackles to rise.

Charley Conley rode back in my life.

CHAPTER FIFTEEN

"Charles Conley," Mama declared with a radiant smile as she stepped outside, wiping her hands on the apron. "My, don't you look dashing." Her voice would have made me think that Colonel Rip Ford, dressed in his Sunday-go-to-meetings, had come to pay us a call. Had she not said his name, however, I never would have known that stout figure in buckskins, riding an Indian pony was my old enemy from those Jacksboro school days.

Dashing? With a bulge of tobacco in his beard-covered cheek, a Smith carbine in one hand, and a brace of Navy Colt revolvers tucked in the green sash strapped around his waist, he looked a rogue.

Fifteen years old, I figured, and already standing six-foot-four and weighing two hundred pounds. His knuckles resembled walnuts, his hair hung long, greasy, uncombed, and he wore a slouch hat filled with at least a half dozen holes, topped off with a buzzard feather attached to a hatband made from rattlesnake skin. Charley probably believed that superstition held by folks that rattler skin headbands kept you from getting headaches.

"Ma'am." One hand held the reins to his piebald gelding, the other gripped the carbine, so he raised the .50-caliber Smith's barrel to tip his hat brim as the buzzard feather fluttered in the breeze.

He nodded at Uncle Moses. Reluctantly he gave me a similar greeting, but said nothing to either of us.

It looked like a badly shaped piece of clay that had been thrown onto his face, slightly off center—which was Charley Conley's nose. Scars lined his knotted forehead and his massive, filthy hands. I rubbed my cheeks, knowing that I could not detect even the beginning fuzz of a beard, while looking at Charley's, thick, dark, dirty one.

"Capt'n said I should come by here when the Comanch' moon come up," Charley told my mother.

"I did not know you were working for Ben Earnhardt," Mama said.

"Ain't." Charley turned to send a waterfall of tobacco juice splattering on the ground. He faced Mama again, and looked awkward as he tried to wipe his mouth with his sleeve, but could not figure out how to do it with his hands full. "Rangerin'."

As I stared at his shirt sleeves, I almost said something out loud, but Uncle Moses put a hand on my shoulder, hard and firm, and whispered: "Quiet, Top Soldier."

Not hearing Uncle Moses or seeing my reaction, Mama apologized for her self-perceived rudeness. "Light down, Charles. Pierce, will you be so kind as to take Mister Conley's horse to the corral?"

Moses Gage moved first. "I'll take your war bag, Charley. You'll be stayin' with us, I reckon."

"Reckon."

"I did not know Ben Earnhardt was still riding with the Rangers," Mama said as I took the reins from Charley's hand and led the horse away.

"He don't. Much. But Capt'n asked, and, well . . . I'd do anything for him. He was with my daddy when he got kilt at Chickamauga."

Mama said: "I know, Charles. I remember. I remember your mother, too." She sighed, and changed the subject. "And how is your sister Janet, and her new husband Clarke? Do you hear from them? Are they doing well in Comanche Springs?"

Even underneath the mask of sweat-packed dirt, I could see Charley's face darken. "Ma'am," he said, after shifting the quid of tobacco to the other cheek, "I ain't got no sister."

The smile on Mama's face vanished, and several seconds passed before she recovered. Her instructions were brief, as she turned to go back inside, saying: "Wash up, Charles. Supper will be ready directly."

I could not forget the image of the upper sleeves of Charley's filthy shirt. Shining black trophies, stitched into the buckskin with sinew.

They were two scalps, Kiowa or Comanche, I assumed.

Mama, being Mama, dished out a vinegar pie for our guest, and we ate the last of Uncle Moses's venison backstrap, with fresh cornbread and stewed carrots for supper.

In the closeness of our house, I learned something else about Charley. He stank.

From that meal on, as long as Charley was with us, we would drag our table outside in the early morning for breakfast and keep it there through the end of supper. It had been Mama's idea, saying the days were so pleasant we should eat outside—actually the days felt hotter than August.

Yet that first night was different.

Inside the house, we ate in silence, because Charley's dismissal of his sister had spoiled Mama's good humor. I had never felt such a dark mood while we ate. Even Mama's cornbread, sweet from the sugar she used but with a kick from cayenne pepper, did not settle easily in my stomach.

When he finished eating, Charley did not ask for seconds. He slurped up the last of his coffee, wiped his mouth and beard with the sleeve of his buckskin shirt, and rose, knocking his chair over. He picked it up without an apology, gave Mama a terse nod while completely ignoring Uncle Moses and me.

"Thank you, ma'am," he said. "Iffen you needs me, I'll be out yonder."

Mama's nod seemed forced. "Breakfast will be . . ."

"Don't eat no breakfast, ma'am. Before daylight, I'll cut a circle up north, look for sign. Back here 'round noon. But I don't eat no dinner, neither. Supper's fine. Ma'am." He tipped the hat he had not removed in our home, and went outside.

"He's meaner than he was when he was at school," I said immediately.

"Pierce." Mama did not care for insulting houseguests, behind their backs or to their faces.

"What did he mean saying he doesn't have a sister?" I asked. "Is Janet dead or something?"

"Eat that last bit of cornbread," Uncle Moses ordered.

"But Papa always . . ."

"Eat it."

I did, though I did not enjoy it, especially having seen Charley Conley break off a chunk with his filthy hands.

I was no dunce. Charley Conley and Uncle Moses were here for protection. We called a full moon a Comanche moon, because the Indians were prone to raid then, especially between spring and fall, when their ponies were well fed.

Even with Hog Clagett, Ellis Morrell, and many other hired men on the trail to Abilene, Ben Earnhardt still had a plenty of hands to keep an eye out for his wife and the horses and bulls at his place. The Earnhardt home had been made of stone, two stories high with a cellar, along with portholes for firing guns and shutters six inches thick. Some folks called his home The Alamo, but practically everyone in Jack County doubted that Santa Anna could have stormed it.

Luckily Conley did not spend much time around our home. He was gone the next morning before I went outside to do my chores, and I would not see him until that pinto horse brought him back late in the afternoon. Uncle Moses, however, always stayed close.

"Look at that sorry horse," I told Uncle Moses once when I spotted Charley, riding in from a distance. "You wouldn't catch me dead on a pinto."

Chuckling, he continued to pump the bellows as we worked on fashioning horseshoes. "You sound like Capt'n Earnhardt."

I wiped the sweat off my forehead with my bandanna. "Never seen a good cowboy yet on an Indian pony," I said.

"Charley Conley ain't no cowboy," Uncle Moses said as he pulled out a shoe, placed it on the anvil, and began hammering, sending sparks showering across the workplace.

"That's for damn' sure," I agreed.

"Watch your tongue, Top Soldier. Your mama wouldn't like it. Comes to think on it . . . I don't care much for it, neither."

Frowning, I looped the bandanna around my neck, although I did not tie the ends, as I knew I'd need it to wipe away the accumulation of sweat.

As I shifted, I could see a piebald gelding coming in to our yard. Like most Texans, I had developed a prejudice against pintos, having heard Captain Earnhardt and many others belittle such animals, although I do not recall Papa ever saying a word for or against piebalds or skewbalds.

Steam hissed as Uncle Moses dunked the shoe into a bucket of water. When he brought it out, he stepped around me and looked out at the horse and rider. "I don't know, Top Soldier," he said. "Looks like a pretty good bit of horseflesh if you ask me."

We saw no Indians that spring or summer, except a few tame Tonkawa scouts now and then when we rode into Jacksboro for supplies. Uncle Moses, of course, had explained that best. "You don't see a Comanch' or Kiowa unless he wants to be seen. Then, often times, it's too late to do nothin' 'bout it."

By then, the Army had moved out of Jacksboro proper, and had begun building a post along Lost Creek that they called Fort Richardson. The bluebellies had tried to establish a fort at Buffalo Springs, only to give up on that one because of the lack of water and the rough country. Richardson itself wasn't much to look at, at least not in the spring of '68. Construction had only started back in late November, so Fort Richardson was made up mostly of Sibley tents and picket houses, erected quickly and shoddily, although the powder house was made with thick walls. So was the stockade. And the Yanks were working on another big stone building.

Uncle Moses and I took a buckboard in for supplies one morning and rode past the fort. Standing on the road between the post and town stood Nancy Livermore, still in pigtails, though now I stood a good two inches taller than she did. She was still watching the soldier boys.

"Howdy, Miss Nancy," Uncle Moses said as he pulled on the lines to stop the two mules.

"Hi." She grinned, and pointed at the fort. "That's Fort Richardson."

"Yes, it is," Uncle Moses said.

"I hear they're lettin' colored boys in the Army," she said. "A corporal told me. Says some are stationed at Fort Sill, wherever that is."

"Up in Indian Territory," Uncle Moses said.

"Have you heard that? About the colored boys?"

He nodded. "Indeed I have."

"Why don't you join?"

Uncle Moses laughed. "I reckon them generals and majors want a fellow much younger than me, Miss Nancy. How's your pappy?"

"Fine." She looked at me. "You gonna join?"

"And be a Yankee?" I shook my head. "Hardly."

"They ain't bad sorts," she said. "Corporal Newton's real nice. So's this captain. They're in the Sixth Cavalry."

I looked at the beehive of workers. Although I did like rocks, I could not see myself putting up a bunch of stone buildings where officers would be living while the enlisted men stayed in those dismal picket houses. I figured I had built my last home, and it stood near twelve miles downstream.

"Corporal Newton says it was named after a Union general," Nancy said. "He was killed at Antietam."

"Antietam?" I echoed. Nancy had finally gotten my interest. That was the Yankee name of the battle we called Sharpsburg. Papa had fought there. I had heard Captain Earnhardt mention it several times, and Horace Butler once or twice, even if Horace's regiment had not been at that particular fight. Bobby Weatherly's older brother had died there.

"Uhn-huh," Nancy said. She looked back at the soldiers. "Corporal Newton was there, but, back then, he wasn't a corporal but a captain. Can you believe that?"

I muttered something.

"How's your finger, Top Soldier?" Nancy asked. Even in Jacksboro, my nickname had become so common it felt as though no one remembered my given name.

I held it up for her inspection.

"That's gross," she said. "Corporal Newton . . . he lost a finger at Antietam. He says I should call him Jeremy, but Pa and Ma won't let me. They won't let me do nothing." She cocked her head, and stared at my finger, adding: "Maybe that's why he can't be a captain any more, on account of his missing finger. It's his pinky finger, though, not like yours, and it doesn't look gross . . . on him."

Uncle Moses tipped his hat, and I followed suit, and the mules continued on toward town, leaving Nancy Livermore staring at the Yankees at work.

"Some help those bluecoats are," I said with contempt as I stared at my scarred finger. I didn't think it was gross. "Act more like carpenters than soldiers."

"Not all of 'em, Top Soldier," Uncle Moses said. "Place is to hold five companies, so they needs some roofs over their heads. And they be plenty of horse betwixt here and Fort Sill, maybe even off toward the Llano Estacado. Protectin' you, your ma, and me."

The Army post wasn't the only thing growing in these parts. Jacksboro itself had grown. Two saloons greeted us as we crossed the bridge into town. You would find no more vacant lots, and Rat Row had evolved into a vibrant part of town. We passed the cribs and the gambling parlors and the saloons that had sprung up to satisfy the needs of the Yankee soldiers. Nancy Livermore's father's Wichita Saloon, which had been serving grog for as long as I could remember, now had plenty of competition when it came to selling liquor and beer: Union Headquarters, The First

National, The Last Chance, Little Shamrock, and many with no names other than Saloon or Beer & Whiskey. One soddy even had a non-nonsense sign, painted crudely, and attached to a post by the canvas door: GET DRUNK HERE.

Why some of these new places even displayed signs out front proclaiming that they offered free sandwiches, goober peas, and pickles.

Jim Fountain's father had opened a hat shop, but, if you believed what we heard at Mr. Goldman's store, most of the hats he sold were those he collected off the streets in front of the saloons after the Army payroll had reached Fort Richardson.

A two-story stone courthouse was being built in town, which now boasted three mercantiles, four barbershops, a bank, two wagon yards, and even an apothecary. We passed Miss Linda Riley's schoolhouse, although it was empty as this was Saturday.

"Miss it, Top Soldier?" Uncle Moses asked as we rode by the now whitewashed building.

I stared at it, but I answered with a scoff: "School?"

"Yeah. School. Miss it?"

I turned back to look at the mules. You just could not lie to Moses Gage. "Yeah," I conceded. "Sometimes."

"Well, maybe one of these days, your folks'll let you go back. Boy needs an education." He gestured behind us. "And them blue boys, they might help you get back to them books and such."

Although Captain Earnhardt had said we could get better prices at Wilson's Store, we remained loyal to Mr. Goldman, so that's where Uncle Moses stopped.

"Is it true?" I asked as he set the brake.

"Is what true, Top Soldier?"

"What Nancy said . . . about the Army letting men of color like yourself join up."

"Plenty fought and died during the Rebellion, Top Soldier. We're free now. So, yep, it's true."

He climbed down on one side, and I leaped off the other, fishing the list Mama had given me out of my pocket.

"Why didn't you fight?" I asked. "In the war, I mean."

"Wasn't none of my affair."

"Wasn't Papa's either," I said. "Probably wasn't even Corporal Jeremy Newton's," I added, saying his name with as much derision as I could muster.

Uncle Moses laughed. "Top Soldier, I declare, you are jealous."

"Not by a damned sight," I said, and, this time, he did not object to my profanity. He didn't laugh, either.

CHAPTER SIXTEEN

During those years, my moods swung like the pendulum on the big clock in Ezra Goldman's store. I'd be happy, then angry, at practically anyone—Nancy Livermore, Corporal Jeremy Newton, Mama, Papa, Captain Earnhardt, even Moses Gage. But mostly myself.

I grew. I ate. I worked. I read.

I thought about the war, now over for more than three years, and thought about the stories I had never gotten to hear from Papa. Sometimes I even wished he had been killed, like Bobby Weatherly's big brother. Then I hated myself for such a wicked, unchristian thought.

A week and a half after my visit to town, Papa and Horace Butler rode up in new duds, and on new horses. Mama ran outside, as if she had sensed Papa was home, and as Horace led the two horses to the corral, Papa and Mama whirled in a warm embrace in the summer dust.

"Hey, Top Soldier!" Papa yelled. "You've grown." He let loose of Mama and walked toward me, the spurs chiming on his new, but dusty, black boots. Pulling off a stained glove, he held out his hand. "Reckon you are too big for a kiss now."

"Yes, sir," I told him, and we shook. I expected

him to pull me into a hug anyway, but he did not. Instead, he untucked his shirt, and began removing a belt strapped tight against his stomach. It was heavy, and I could hear the clinking of coins as he extended the belt out to Mama.

"Here you go, Martha," he said.

She laid it on the table that sat soaking up the late afternoon sun. When Mama opened it, and reached inside, her hand came back empty. Her face had paled, and she turned back at Papa.

"Why there's . . . it's . . . I can't . . . ," Mama stammered.

Papa grinned. "Forty a head, Martha. *Forty dollars a head!*"

Over supper, Horace Butler did most of the talking. Papa grinned, while Mama, Charley Conley, Uncle Moses, and I sat rapt, often with our jaws open. Stories about stampedes and lightning storms . . . Indians demanding a toll for crossing their reservation . . . a tornado well off in the distance—the first, despite living in Texas, that Papa or Horace Butler had ever seen. And all about Abilene, the Sodom and Gomorrah of Kansas.

"You ain't seen Jacksboro of late, Mister Braden," Uncle Moses said, "if you think Abilene's wicked."

Mama sliced the half-pound cake she had made with lemon icing.

"What about 'em Injuns?" Charley Conley asked. "That demanded you pay 'em?"

Papa answered: "We paid them."

"You paid an Injun?" Charley gasped.

"Ten beeves. It was their land."

Horace added: "We figured if we didn't pay 'em, they might set the prairie afire, or stampede the herd."

"I never would 'a' paid no Injun," Charley said as he grabbed the plate of cake. "Nothin'." Shunning a fork, he ate the cake with his fingers, his rough beard catching the crumbs. I figured he'd snack on them later.

"Ben didn't want to, either," Papa said. "But we did."

"Forty dollars a head?" Charley said. "Ten beeves? That was a smart of money. No, I'd never pay no Injun." He drank the last of his coffee, and stood, tipping the hat that I had rarely seen leave his head. "Missus Braden. Thank you for your hospitality, but I reckon I should get back to Belknap."

"Charles, it's late. Stay here tonight," Mama said.

"Plenty of daylight left. No, ma'am, but I thank you. Thank you-all. I'll ride out."

We rose and waited for him to pack his possibles and mount the piebald. He nodded again, and headed to the creek, turned his horse, and rode for Jacksboro. He'd probably stop at one of the twenty-seven—I had counted them—saloons in town that night. Get drunk. Lose his hat, though I doubted Mr. Fountain would try to resell it, considering its shabby condition. Then return to Fort Belknap the next day, or whenever he sobered up.

After he had left, Papa led us back to the table to finish our cake and let Horace tell a few more stories.

"Martha," Papa asked, "do I smell as bad as Charley?"

She smiled. "Well, Wil," she answered, "you and Horace could stand a bath."

"But Missus Braden," Horace Butler said, "we got a good washin' in Abilene. Cost me twenty-five cents."

With Papa's newfound wealth from the sale of the herd in Abilene, chickens and a rooster returned to our ranch. We had not had chickens since the raid on our home during the late war, and the only eggs I had tasted since Austin had been quail eggs. It was my job to build the coop.

Some of the money Papa deposited in the new bank in Jacksboro, but he did not totally trust banks—which would save us from some grief years later when the Panic of 1873 finally reached Jack County—so most of the Liberty Head double eagles, many of them freshly minted, were put in Mason jars—another invention by some Yankee tinsmith—and buried underneath the leftover flagstone we now moved closer to the house.

Another portion of the money was used for buying three goats, two of which I would have to milk, a pair of boots from the new cobbler in Jacksboro for me, a day dress for Mama, the color of magenta with wide pagoda sleeves, a brindle-colored longhorn bull, and a Winchester Yellow Boy, the 1866 Model repeating rifle, chambered for the .44 Henry rimfire cartridges, which got its nickname from the shiny frame made of a bronze alloy. Papa treated himself to a Howard key-wind watch, gold-plated with a hunting case. A gift for Mama arrived in August, freighted in a heavy wagon by three Negroes and a white man with a gray beard.

"Wil!" Mama gasped once the workers had lowered the massive surprise off the wagon and removed the canvas tarp that had protected it over the long miles from the steamboat wharf in Jefferson, far over in East Texas.

It was a Steinway, a square piano—not an upright and not as large as a grand—made of carved Brazilian rosewood, and came with a matching stool.

"Looks like a fat man's coffin," I said.

Papa laughed, but Mama frowned, shaking her head at my joke and announcing: "It is beautiful, Wil. Beautiful."

I didn't think it would fit in the house, or through

the doorway, but those workers performed magic. So did Mama, when she cleared a space for it next to the fireplace. Papa paid the white man in gold, and once they were on their way, Mama eased down on the stool.

"I didn't know you played piano, Mama," I said.

"I haven't since leaving North Carolina," she said, "but I do. And so will you."

I didn't, though. Oh, Mama tried to give me lessons, but I was twelve years old, and then thirteen, and then fourteen, and I would often complain that my finger hurt when she tried to teach me where to place my fingers on the keys. Eventually she gave up.

She played beautifully: Liszt's *Mephisto Waltzes*, Bach's Fantasia in F sharp Minor, Beethoven's Piano Sonata No. 10 in G Major, or popular songs like "Wait for the Wagon," anything by Stephen Foster, or the Russian "Kalinka."

To this day, it is one of my biggest regrets that I did not learn.

What Papa surprised me with, though, I cherished, even if it was not new. Papa unwrapped the revolver, a Colt, and handed it to me. It felt as heavy as the gold-filled money belt Papa had worn from Abilene to Jack County.

"It's a Dragoon," he said. "Forty-Four caliber. Time you learned how to shoot it."

"Did you carry it in the war, Papa?" I asked,

feeling how cold the steel was, in contrast to the warmth of the walnut grip.

He laughed. "I was infantry. No revolvers for some foot soldier like me. Besides, I wouldn't want to carry that thing. Weighs a ton."

That was the most he had ever spoken of the war to me.

"What was . . . ?"

Papa cut me off. "This has the balls." He dropped the dark leather pouch, heavy with lead, on the table, and withdrew a copper flask from the back pocket of his trousers. "This holds the powder." Then a small brass cylinder, with a small lanyard ring at the top, he laid between the powder flask and the bullet pouch. I could make out the word **IMPROVED** at the top. "This is the capper." Most percussion cappers I had seen were straight.

We walked to the banks of Lost Creek, where he showed me how to load the pistol, how to cap it, and how to shoot it. "Hold it with both hands, Top Soldier. Spread out your feet. This is basically a cannon. It'll knock you on your butt and the barrel will come up and break your nose, if you're not careful."

He fired first, and then handed the Colt to me.

"It was my father's," he said. "Now it's yours."

I squeezed off a shot, and missed the stone on the other side of the creek by a good fifty feet. My ears rang, and my hand hurt from the kick of the .44, but I grinned.

"I'll need to make a belt and holster," I told him, "so I can carry it with me when I go to Abilene with you next year."

"We'll see," he said. "But I'd advise you to carry it in the chuckwagon. Not on your hip."

Three freighters were killed and scalped along the road to Decatur that summer, and just before fall, a soldier was found riddled with arrows near the government sawmill. Two soldiers had been killed in skirmishes with hostile Indians. Many more, locals and strangers, however, died in Jacksboro itself, in gun brawls, knife fights, or fisticuffs. Several horses were stolen during a Comanche moon, and two of Luke Caldwell's prized bulls were found butchered, south toward the Palo Pinto country.

We escaped harm, though, and, all in all, 1868 passed as not a bad year.

Until winter came, and Captain Earnhardt brought a newspaper from Illinois—a drummer had left it behind on the Fort Worth to Fort Belknap stagecoach—which told of an Indian attack along the Washita River.

It had happened around Thanksgiving, although we did not learn of it until just after Christmas. Townsfolk had heard, of course, since they lived next door to the soldiers at Fort Richardson, but we had not been to Jacksboro in quite some time.

Papa folded the paper, as Captain Earnhardt

said: "That's a hundred and fifty red devils we don't have to worry about no more, Wil."

"Cheyenne women and children it says here," Papa said, and handed the paper over to Mama.

The captain spit into the cuspidor. "Yankee paper. They ain't got Comanch' killin' their neighbors in Illinois. I got to hand it to that Yankee Custer, though. He done square by me."

Mama sank into the chair. "Women and children," she said, shaking her head.

"Well." Captain Earnhardt rubbed his eye patch, and tipped his hat. "At least they won't be marryin' no sons of white folk."

The battle—if one could call it that—was against a peaceful village of mostly Cheyenne Indians in the western part of Indian Territory, led by a chief named Black Kettle who had escaped a similar massacre in Colorado at Sand Creek in 1864. He did not survive this one.

It had been led by George Custer, who I remembered as the dashing, energetic young officer I had met back in Austin shortly after the war. The man with the fetching wife and those great hounds.

The Washita made Custer famous as an Indian fighter. It did not, however, make him popular in the Braden household.

"Wil?" Mama asked. "What will this mean?"

"The Cheyennes aren't enemies to the Kiowas and Comanches," Papa said. "You slaughter

Cheyenne women and children, it's apt to be like kicking open a hornet's nest all across the Southern Plains."

Which it did, though mostly north of Indian Territory in western Kansas and eastern Colorado Territory, not in North Texas. And not in winter.

Eventually spring returned to Jack County, and Captain Earnhardt began preparing for another drive. I worked harder in the gather this time than I had in '68. I found myself branding steers, but not using the Rafter B iron. Everything we road branded that spring was for Captain Earnhardt.

"Papa?" I asked one night after Mama finished playing *The Blue Danube*, the music for which she had had to beg Mr. Goldman to find. "Why haven't we branded any of our calves?"

He sat at the table, cleaning his fingernails with a pocket knife. "Ben runs a right smart more cattle than we do, Top Soldier."

That much everyone in Jack County knew. Captain Earnhardt had fared much better in Kansas in 1868 than we had, and, since then, he had bought out the Diamond 4, near Antelope, and even brought in a herd of two hundred steers from just east of Weatherford.

"Ben's running another two thousand head to Abilene," he said. "I'm letting our herd grow."

My heart sank. "Are we going with him?" I

223

asked, my voice filled with hope, although I already knew the answer.

Mama turned around on her piano stool. She knew the answer, too, but she had known it a lot longer than I had.

"I told Ben we'd watch after his place," Papa said. "Lot of Indian trouble up north since that ruction along the Washita. And I'd rather stay close to home this year."

"Then why are we helping him?" I sang out, angry. I had my grandfather's Dragoon .44, new boots, all ten fingers working. I had toiled all spring, smelling burning hide, eating what Solomon Burke called food, and washing it down with miserable coffee. I wanted to see Abilene. I wanted a lot.

"Because he's our neighbor," Papa said calmly. "And he asked us."

"He asked *you*," I said, and stormed out of the house.

"Pierce!" his voice thundered, but the noise of the slamming door cut him off, and I moved straight toward the woodpile, where I grabbed an axe and began chopping.

"Wil," I heard Mama say, and she must have stopped him. Likely that was a good thing. I chopped until darkness fell, and afterward I sat alone on the chopping block.

Moods. That's how I explain it now. Being a teenager in a hard land.

Back then I had decided something. Papa did not want to drive our herd to Kansas because of the Indian troubles up north. He was a coward. That's why he didn't ever talk about the war. It still frightened him.

I had seen what had happened when Horace Butler had gotten into a fight. That had been a week earlier, when a cowboy had made some comment about Horace and some chippie he had met in Jacksboro in the rough part of town, south of Mr. Livermore's Wichita Saloon.

"Yeah, I lost the fight," Horace admitted to Mama when she sliced off a slab of beef to put over his black eye, "but I sure whupped him of a bad habit."

Horace Butler would fight. I knew Captain Earnhardt would. By Jacks, even I had fought Charley Conley, twice. Why those miserable bluecoats at Fort Richardson had fought. But not my father.

Those moods of mine did not lighten over the months. Captain Earnhardt rode north late in April with two thousand longhorns, while Papa, Horace, and I worked our spread. Uncle Moses, and even Charley Conley, rode by during the Comanche moon to stay and help if needed.

My understanding of that made me despise Papa. Last year it would have made sense. Papa and Horace were riding north to Kansas with Captain Earnhardt. We needed extra guns and men, in case the Comanches or Kiowas attacked. But this year? Papa was here. Horace Butler was here. We had a brand-spanking new Winchester repeater. And I had my grandfather's .44-caliber Dragoon. We did not need Uncle Moses's help. Most certainly we did not need Charley Conley, or his stink.

More soldiers died. More cattle were killed. A family of homesteaders down along the Brazos was butchered, burned out, and buried. Freighters hauling corn to Fort Griffin, another new Yankee post a mile or so west of the Clear Fork of the Brazos, had been attacked, leaving six men dead. But our house remained untouched.

I gave that credit to Uncle Moses, and, grudgingly, even Charley Conley—not Papa.

Captain Earnhardt returned even richer. Papa assured me that we would make another drive— he did not say when—and that I'd go with him. But by then, I did not care.

Four times during the summer, Captain Earnhardt rode into the yard with Uncle Moses and plenty of armed men. Charley Conley was even with him once.

Earnhardt would go on about how Indians had raided someone or killed some stock or stolen some horses. He always ended with: "Wil, we could use you and that ol' Enfield you stole from me."

Although Papa still had that old weapon, he

would grab the Yellow Boy, saddle his horse, and ride off with the posse. They never came close to catching the Indians, though, and Papa never fired a shot.

Which figured in my mind, because I knew Uncle Moses had told me that you never see Indians, unless they want to be seen. Papa knew that. He rode with Ben Earnhardt because he knew there would be no fighting, no chance of getting hurt. And, every time those Indian hunters came to our house, I longed for them to ask me to ride with them.

But I remained behind, always, hearing Papa's voice: "Stay close, Top Soldier." That would echo in my head until the men returned with worn-out mounts and no scalps. And no glory.

So I hunted for fossils and rocks, and I did my chores. I fished in Lost Creek. When we did the fall gather, I rode, roped, and branded. Around the campfires, I listened to cowhands who had fought in the war brag about their exploits. One said he had shot a Yankee cardsharp dead in Abilene for cheating him. Nobody called him a liar.

Trees lost their leaves, and winter set in, cold and angry, wet and miserable. I worked on my Reader, mended tack, and broke holes into the ice so the horses and cattle could drink.

I brooded.

Until New Year's Day, when Uncle Jake returned.

PART III
1870

CHAPTER SEVENTEEN

A blue norther blew in that afternoon, dropping the temperature forty degrees in three hours and darkening the sky as we rode from the range to our home. By the time Horace Butler and Papa had the horses in the corral and barn, and I had rounded up the chickens and covered the coop, those ominous clouds opened up, and sleet began pelting me.

Our chores completed, we raced across the frozen ground, spurs jingling, ice crunching, and stopped underneath our porch roof to dump the sleet off our hats before Mama opened the door and told us to hurry inside.

"Some new year, huh?" Horace joked as he unbuckled his chaps.

"It's moisture," said Papa, ever the rancher, as he took the steaming mug of coffee that Mama handed him.

Once out of my boots, I shimmied out of my leggings, hanging them on the peg underneath my hat. Mama had made hot chocolate, a treat for the new year, so I took my mug, and walked to the window. The panes had already frosted over.

"I can't see a thing," I said.

"Don't worry, Top Soldier," Horace told me. "Comanch' don't ride in this weather."

"No one should," Mama said, and went back to finish cooking our New Year's Day meal.

The rest of the day we spent by the fireplace with Papa hitching a horsehair rope, Horace Butler mending a saddle, and me darning socks. Mama had kept complaining, though slightly in jest, that all I did was grow out of my duds and wear holes in my socks. She would say that she couldn't stop me from growing, but she could make me ease her workload by darning my own socks. I didn't care much for that chore, but I knew better than to object, or lie that it made my finger hurt.

By candlelight and the glow of the fireplace, we ate—cornbread, fried beefsteaks, boiled carrots and potatoes, with lemon cake for dessert. Then we returned to our chores, listening to the sleet pelting the roof while Mama cleaned the dishes and set the batter for tomorrow's breakfast.

By the time Mama had retired from the kitchen to inspect my socks, Papa had set his lariat on the floor and pushed himself out of his chair.

"You hear something, Horace?" he asked.

Now drawing a monthly salary, Horace looked up, licking his lips and holding his long needle threaded with sinew.

All I could hear was the rhythmic tapping of the sleet, which had slackened, but not stopped.

Papa had always been blessed by an extraordinary set of ears, and he started reaching over the fireplace mantel for the Winchester Yellow Boy, when someone began banging on the door—which startled Mama.

"You-all had better be home and not dancing at Captain Earnhardt's!"

Our heavy door, the sleet, and the wind muffled the voice, but Papa started laughing as he replaced the rifle on its hooks. "That crazy fool," he said, and moved to lift the bar.

"Goodness, gracious," Mama said as the heavily bundled figure stepped inside, dripping sleet on our floor.

Horace Butler and I remained in our chairs, shooting each other curious glances before focusing on the tall figure shrugging out of a heavy, caped greatcoat, and slapping a black slouch hat against his chaps.

"Jacob!" Mama exclaimed. "Are you crazy?"

Before he could answer, Mama had raced off to the wash basin in the kitchen area to find a clean tin mug, then she returned to the fireplace and grabbed the coffee pot resting on the hearth.

"It has been debated," my uncle said.

Papa added—" 'Course, he's crazy"—as he gathered the coat from the floor, hung it on a rack, and went to fetch the mug from Mama while our visitor pulled off his boots and chaps.

The last time I had seen him had been almost five years ago, and what I recalled most vividly were his brilliant blue eyes. The eyes were the same, full of life and fire. In no way did he resemble the man who had made Mama faint back in 1865.

His pants were like those favored by the Mexican *vaqueros* I had seen from time to time, dark-blue striped, with *peso* buttons from knee to hem down the side, lined with crimson piping, and the seat and thighs padded with black leather. His shirt was black, laced up with a strip of rawhide, and he wore a scarlet scarf and doeskin gloves. He had replaced that sorry excuse for a hat with a black Stetson, low-crowned and flat-brimmed, and his boots, custom-made no doubt, gleamed black, inlaid with white stars in the uppers. Strapped across his waist was a fine belt, with Colt Navy revolvers holstered butt-forward on each hip.

Papa offered Uncle Jake the cup of coffee—we had finished the chocolate—and his hand in greeting, but my uncle ignored both, and stepped around his older brother.

"I didn't freeze my tail off all the way from Jacksboro to see you on this glorious evening," he said.

Immediately he swung my mother into his arms, and danced her around the room, Mama laughing hysterically, his spurs singing as they whirled. Papa just shook his head, while Horace and I wondered what was going on.

They stopped in front of me, and Uncle Jake

turned around, grinning, holding out his still-gloved right hand. "Put it here, Top Soldier," he said. "It's been a spell."

I did the first thing to come to my mind. I tried to hide the socks and the yarn.

Uncle Jake's thick beard was gone and now he sported a well-groomed mustache and under-lip beard.

When my right hand met his, he gripped it tightly, jerked me to my feet, and crushed me in a bear hug. Almost immediately he pushed me back at arm's length, making me stand in front of my chair. His eyes took in everything about me, and when he released his grip, he looked at my beaming mother and said: "By thunder, Martha, what the devil have you been feeding this boy? He's practically as tall as I am."

Which was far from the case, even with my uncle standing in his stocking feet.

He stepped toward Horace Butler, and held out his hand. "Name's Jake." He hooked a thumb toward Papa. "This ugly cuss's brother."

Horace slowly stood, and they shook as Horace introduced himself. My uncle sat, removing the shiny spurs before Mama made him do so—though he dumped them unceremoniously atop the pie safe—and finally shook Papa's hand and accepted the coffee mug.

"Would you like something to eat?" Mama asked.

"What I'd like," Jacob Braden said, "is something to drink . . . and a wee bit stronger than coffee."

The storm passed, the weather warmed, the ice melted.

I never really knew if Uncle Jake just rode up from South Texas on a whim, of if Papa had invited him, or even why he came, but he stayed on, sleeping in the new bunkhouse Papa had hired carpenters to build.

Although he tried, Jacob Braden proved to everyone that working cattle would never be his forte, but he showed himself to be a master when it came to breaking horses. With Captain Earnhardt planning another drive to Kansas later that year, we had plenty of horses to gentle.

Papa, Uncle Moses, Horace, Uncle Jake, and I built a round pen that winter. I became Uncle Jake's helper.

Sometime in February, when it appeared that winter had passed—at least for the time being, though in Texas you never can tell, both then and now—Captain Earnhardt brought in ten ponies for Uncle Jake to break. Two other riders, men I did not know, rode with the captain, and they all stayed for supper.

When we all had finished the ham, turnips, eggs, and vinegar pie, Papa fetched a brown jug from the bunkhouse.

Whiskey filled the coffee mugs, and Captain Earnhardt raised his. "To John Bell Hood and the First Texas," the captain said.

Mugs lifted, and Papa said softly: "All that's left of them."

They drank.

The next toast came from Horace Butler: "To Terry's Texas Rangers. That's the outfit I fit with."

The captain gruntcd something that sounded like a snigger, but he and the others joined Horace in raising their cups.

I had been helping Mama dry the dishes, but now I walked away from the wash basin, and stood, staring at the men gathered around the fireplace. Mama did not object, for our task had been completed, and shc came behind me and put her hands on my shoulders.

The red-mustached man with a patched denim vest sang out: "You-all recollect that time . . . where was it? 'Round South Mountain?" Every-one stared at him, but no one answered. He went on: "Ol' Bobby Lee? That time he arrested Gen'ral Hood for some silly thing, and Bobby Lee kept Hood in the back of the column? Remember?"

"Oh, yeah." Captain Earnhardt's head bobbed.

The red-mustached man chuckled. "So here comes Bobby Lee . . . and he's ridin' Traveller . . . I swear it on the Good Book . . . and you recollect what you done, Capt'n?"

Earnhardt chuckled. "Ain't likely to forget it. I lift my hat and I yell at General Lee . . . 'Give us Hood!' "

"That's right!" The red-mustached man slapped his thigh. "That's right. And then Conn Conley, he yells out the same thing. 'Give us Hood!' And that done it. And then we's all yellin' it. And Bobby Lee, he reins up, and he stares at us, and he says, he says . . . you-all recollect what he said?"

Uncle Jake answered: " 'You shall have him, gentlemen.' "

"That's right," the red-mustached man said. "That's right. We got him. We got Gen'ral Hood out of the calaboose, or wherever they was a-keepin' him." He turned toward Horace Butler and said: "Bet you-all never done nothin' like that with your Rangers."

"Hey, Red," Uncle Jake said, "you ever see a dead cavalryman?"

They laughed, all but Horace, who shook his head, and said: "All right, fellas. I've heard that joke many a time."

"It's still a good one," Red said.

"That ain't all to that story," Captain Earnhardt said, and everyone fell silent. "Because when General Hood rode back up to meet with General Lee, Lee told Hood that he will be released if he would apologize. And Hood, by Jacks, he shook his head and told Gen'ral Lee that he would not. Said it was on account of his honor as a soldier. And Lee, he nods his head, and he says . . . 'That's all right, General.' He said that when there was fightin' to be done, he wanted Hood and us Texans, and he said that the arrest was suspended."

"You got it done, Capt'n," Red Mustache said.

"Not I," Earnhardt said. "All of us. That's why we had Hood leadin' us on that glorious but God-awful day."

Silence filled the room for several minutes. Red shook his head sadly, and said in a reverent whisper: "Sharpsburg."

"If ever there was hell on earth," added the other rider, a pockmarked man with only the thumb and forefinger on his left hand.

As he refreshed his and a few other cups with the corn whiskey, Uncle Jake slowly began rubbing his left leg.

"One of our ponies prove too much for you?" the pockmarked man asked with a snort that might have been a laugh. Now that I look back on it, I guess he was trying to change the subject.

"Nope," Uncle Jake replied. "Leg always bothers me when there's a change in the air. Yankee canister, courtesy of a bluecoat at Sharpsburg."

"Liked to have planted you that day," Captain Earnhardt said.

"Yanks planted a good deal of us," Uncle Jake said.

The captain let out a mirthless laugh. "That's

certain sure." He shook his head, and rubbed the flesh above his eye patch. "I still don't see how we lost that fight."

"We didn't lose it," Red said. "We just didn't win it."

I stood fascinated, finally hearing a story of a battle that my father had been in.

As my uncle sipped his whiskey, he noticed Mama and me.

"How many times have you heard this story, Top Soldier?" he asked.

I answered softly: "Never."

"How's that?" Jake said, and glanced at Papa, who stared thoughtfully at his tin cup. My uncle looked again at me, waiting for my answer.

My head shook. "Never," I said again softly. Mama let go of my shoulders.

"Wil Braden." Uncle Jake turned and laughed at my brother. "You give us Texans a bad name, not bragging and telling lies." Then to me, he said: "Top Soldier, I'll tell you this. I wouldn't be collecting two dollars for each nag the captain brings here if not for your pa."

I stepped closer to the gathering of men. Even Horace Butler sat spellbound, waiting to hear this war story.

"We hadn't eaten in forever," Uncle Jake began. "Battle had been going on for a while, and we were trying to put something in our guts to tide us over."

Red interrupted to let me know: "Was bein' held in reserve, you see, little one."

"Savin' the best for last," the pockmarked man sang out.

Uncle Jake laughed. "Well, we get the call to arms, and we're following General Hood, and he gives us the command, and then all you can hear is that Rebel yell." Then Uncle Jake broke out into that battle cry, which seemed part banshee, part coyote, but certainly nothing human.

"My goodness," Mama said.

Everyone was laughing and then Red and the pockmarked man joined in, giving their renditions of that Rebel yell.

"We tear out of those woods, cross this turnpike," my uncle continued, "and we're charging, screaming, shooting, running past a little church, meeting the Yanks head-on in this pasture next to a cornfield. Bodies lying everywhere before you knew it. We'd cross twenty, thirty, forty rods without touching the ground. Just stepping on bodies. Then we reached the cornfield . . ." He stopped to sip more whiskey.

"Couldn't eat corn for a month after that day," the pockmarked man commented.

" 'Cause we didn't have none to eat," Red said, laughing.

Uncle Jake continued: "We slipped the bridle, boys. That's what we did. Just kept running through that cornfield, gunning down Yanks by the score. Criminy, we had to be a hundred, close to two hundred yards ahead of every other Reb in the army."

"Five hundred yards!" shouted Red.

"Six!" yelled the pockmarked man.

"Boys," Captain Earnhardt said, "even for Texans, that's a stretcher."

Everyone laughed. Everyone except Mama and me. And Papa, who sat in his chair, staring at his coffee cup of whiskey. I don't think he had taken a sip.

"Then the Yanks get smart. And those batteries open up. Canister and double canister." Uncle Jake turned to face his brother. "That's when Wil here done his good deed for the day."

Papa shook his head, but did not look up.

"You see, Martha, you see, Top Soldier . . . one minute I was running, killing, screaming my head off, and then I'm on the ground, and my leg, by thunder, it's on fire. I think it's shot off, and that's not Texas brag."

"I saw the darnedest thing," Red said. "Explosion off to my right, and I look above the smoke, and it's this arm. Just an arm, flyin' above the smoke, and I can't take my eyes off it. I watch it sail up . . . then fall back down."

The pockmarked man held up his mangled left hand. "Reckon I wasn't that bad hurt, after all," he said, and took a drink of his whiskey.

"Well," Uncle Jake said, "I'm on the ground . . .

figure I'm dead, almost want to be dead, my leg's hurting so bad. And then I hear Wil, and he's right beside me, and I can see the blood just pouring from a hole in his shoulder, but he just comes right past me, and he grabs my blouse, and he drags me, drags me, just drags me over all those dead and dying and praying to be dead. Drags me through the fields and back to that little church. Saved my bacon."

Uncle Jake lifted his mug in toast. "You recollect that, Wil?"

Papa raised his eyes. His head slightly moved.

Captain Earnhardt took a long pull from the jug, foregoing the tin cup. "This greenhorn pup of a lieutenant comes up to me after that scrape, and he stares at me, and he says . . . 'Sergeant, where is your command?' And I tell him . . . 'Dead, sir. Dead on the field.'" He passed the jug to Red, who sipped, and passed it on to the pockmarked man.

"Worse day of my life . . . even worse than when I got captured and taken to Point Lookout," Uncle Jake said.

"Till Appomattox," Red said. "When we learnt it was all for naught."

"What did you do with that medal Hood gave you, Wil?" Uncle Jake asked.

Papa shrugged. "It's somewhere, I reckon."

I found myself staring at my humble father, and I can still remember this swelling pride inside me. Papa was a hero. He never talked about it, but he was a hero. I had been wrong about him.

But Captain Earnhardt shattered that moment with a brief statement, which he said with a laugh: "Wil never was the same after that day, was he, boys? Cried ever' day before a fight and after one. Every time."

"That's a lie!"

Mama gasped. Only then did I realize what I had shouted. Every eye turned from their mugs and locked on me. Captain Earnhardt's blazed the most.

"Pierce," Papa said softly. "To bed with you. Now."

When Captain Earnhardt and the men were gone, after Uncle Jake and Horace had retired to the bunkhouse, and after I had heard Mama and Papa talking for the longest while—though I could not make out anything they said—the rungs on the ladder creaked, and Papa came up to the loft guided by the light of a candle.

I pulled up the quilt and buried my head deep into the pillow. I heard him kneel beside my bed. He knew I was awake.

He said: "I'd say you owe Captain Earnhardt an apology."

Without moving, I said: "You didn't really cry, did you, Papa?"

He laughed, which caused me to roll over and

look at him, see his face lit by the candle, smiling. That had a calming effect on me, for I rarely saw him smile.

"Ben Earnhardt's a lot of things, but he's no liar," Papa said. The smile faded. "Crying is human, Top Soldier. It was practically the only sound of humanity I heard during those four bitter years."

I remember those words so clearly now, yet, at the time, I don't think I registered a single one. Later, it would dawn on me that this had to be the letter that Mama had received in Austin, the one that made her cry. I wish she had let me read it. It might have changed how I felt.

He rose, and moved toward the ladder. "When Jake's finished gentling those horses, you'll help him herd them to the Circle E. You'll apologize to Ben Earnhardt."

CHAPTER EIGHTEEN

A few days later, Uncle Jake and I herded the horses—still a mite green—to Captain Earnhardt's spread. February remained warm. All the long ride over, Uncle Jake told me stories—about Gaines's Mill, where cannon shot would leave nothing left of a man but a bloody mist and an ear-piercing, unhuman scream, and Chickamauga, where Charley Conley's father had died and John Bell Hood had lost his right leg.

"Why doesn't Papa tell those stories the way you do?" I asked.

"Wil never was much for gab, Top Soldier," Uncle Jake said. "I taken his share of talking and bragging. I got the good looks, too."

Laughing, I leaned back in the saddle as we slowed the ponies to a walk and listened as he told me about a fight between a Rebel in the 1st Texas named Taylor against a big cuss from Hampton's Legion that went on for six days, and was declared a draw only because the troops had to march out to Second Manassas.

After the mustangs had been delivered and Uncle Jake had been paid, I asked Captain Earnhardt to accept my apology.

"Watch who you call a liar, boy," he told me. "Men have gotten bad hurt, some even buried, for lettin' such a slight slip off a tongue." He offered his hand, and I shook it. "But in my case, I am a liar. And a good one." He smiled. "You ain't an Indian, so I'll let you live. Besides, I need your pa . . . even that scalawag you have for an uncle."

His wife asked if we would sit down for dinner with them, but Uncle Jake swept off that black hat, bowed in the saddle, and said we had business elsewhere. We rode off, but not for home.

The remainder of that day began a period of gallivanting across the countryside with Jacob Braden. We rode to Jacksboro, where we watched the new church being put up—on the far side of town, far away from Fort Richardson and the rough-and-tumble district that had sprung up on that side of town.

✓The ladies present gathered around, and Uncle Jake swept off his hat, and told them toned-down stories about the recent unpleasantness. Jake—he told me to drop the "uncle" as it made him feel like he was either an old man or Moses Gage—agreed that he would attend the first social at the new church. Next we rode to the Wichita Saloon.

I half expected him to leave me outside with the horses crowding the rails, but as soon as he slid from the saddle, he asked: "How old are you now, Top Soldier?"

"Eight- . . . um . . ." I couldn't lie to him. "Fourteen. Almost."

"Well don't grow gray hairs sitting on that piece of glue bait you call a horse," he said. Without waiting, he pushed through the doors, and I quickly followed.

"Two beers," he told Mr. Livermore, who must not have recognized me, or perhaps he did not care who he served, for he drew two beers and slid the foaming mugs down the bar, where Jake caught his and brought it, from smooth practice, to his lips. Me? I spilled a healthy portion of mine before taking a swallow. Jake grabbed a towel to wipe the suds off his mustache.

The beer tasted bitter, and warm, and I let Jake

finish most of mine. He started a conversation with a cowhand standing next to us, and the drover talked of stampedes at midnight, danger on the trail, and a pistol fight he had seen in Abilene that left four men dead.

Then we rode by the fort to watch the Yankees playing soldier boys. Afterward, we went to the post office to check for mail. We visited one of the saloons that served free lunches with drinks, and then Jake spent about twenty or thirty minutes chatting up the freckle-faced blonde who ran the millinery.

The school bell rang, and, thinking about Linda Riley and seeing how preoccupied Jake was with the blonde, I started off in that direction, but stopped when a buggy went past and someone called my name.

Turning, I saw a bluecoat. Beside him sat Nancy Livermore, who called out: "Hello, Top Soldier. Here's a real soldier." Then she stuck out her tongue.

I went back to the hitching rail, grabbed the reins to Nutmeg, and swung into the saddle.

"I'm going home," I told Jake.

He merely waved.

Winter did not return. The days warmed and lengthened, and the countryside greened up.

"Are we going to Kansas this year?" I asked Papa one afternoon.

Papa smoothed his mustache before answering. "Next year maybe."

Mama, who had been feeding the chickens, must have heard, because she came over to explain. "Pierce, we still have money from that first drive . . . I sometimes feel like a whiskey-runner's wife."

Papa added: "We'll have more beeves by next year. Make a drive worth our while."

Well, I had heard that from Horace Butler and Uncle Moses, and even Red at the Circle E Ranch, but I guess I had needed to hear it from Papa. Now I had, so I could ask: "Well, I'd like to hire on with Captain Earnhardt."

He stopped filing a blue roan's hoof, lowered the leg, and stepped around the big gelding. He looked at Mama, then me.

"You ask Ben?" Papa said.

"I plan to," I said, and knew enough to add: "With your permission."

"Ben's not going this year, either, Top Soldier," he said with a sigh.

"But . . ." I looked at the round pen. "We . . . well, Jake . . . we broke all those ponies."

"I know. But Ben got an offer for his steers and those cow ponies from a drover named Pryor. Sold out to him." He took a drink of water, and returned, file in his hand, to the roan. "Next year, Top Soldier."

Once again I decided that my father was

yellow. He had cried after Sharpsburg. He never told war stories. He wouldn't go on trail drives to Kansas. He had no Indian scalps. All he did was work hard. He rarely went into Jacksboro, especially since Jacksboro had gotten bigger and wilder.

I was a teenager, you see, yet I was a child. Jake Braden fit the image I wanted, that I needed. Wild, reckless, full of life, full of stories. So I rode with him every chance I got.

We went fishing—Jake could fish—and we rode to Jacksboro. Oh, I made sure to have my chores done, at least most of them, before I'd lope off with Jake. We went to a ball, a dance, a barn-raising. We stopped in to see that blonde. We visited more than a half-dozen of Jacksboro's watering holes, though I usually opted for coffee or sarsaparilla rather than beer or rye.

It was on one of those rides with Jake that I reined up and reached for the Dragoon I kept in a pommel holster. Jake had trotted a good distance before he realized I no longer rode at his side, or listening to his story about the siege at Knoxville. After stopping his horse, he turned around in the saddle. He started to speak, but stopped. His eyes, which he shielded with his gloved hand, shifted off to the west, the direction in which I was looking.

"Probably a dead cow," he said. "Or calf."

I nodded. "Probably."

The buzzards kept circling.

"Guess we should check it out," he said.

So we rode, keeping our short guns close.

It was neither cow nor calf.

When we told Papa what we had found, he rode out with Uncle Moses and Horace Butler, telling us to finish shoeing the horses. Jacob Braden wasn't much good at that job, either.

"You never shod a horse?" I asked him.

"Top Soldier, down in Harrisburg, the sons of J.J. Braden did not shoe horses. Men did that for us." He studied the finger he had just cut, shaking it, and wiping it with a handkerchief he pulled from his trouser pocket. "Your father used to be just like me . . . a Braden. Now he's . . ." Jake sighed.

I took the hammer and began working on the horse, but soon could no longer do the job. My stomach remained sick. I sweated more than I should. I glanced at the house, fearing that Mama would come out to investigate.

"She was . . . ," I started.

"An Indian," Jake said. "Don't get all worked up about it."

"She was scalped," I said. "And . . ."

"Don't think about it, Top Soldier. I'm trying not to."

"But the baby . . ."

"Top Soldier!" Jake's blue eyes turned icy cold,

and I held my tongue, but I could not forget what I had seen that afternoon.

Still, I went back to the horse, and made myself finish this job.

When Papa returned, Horace was with him, but not Uncle Moses. Neither said anything about Moses Gage, but later I would learn that he had ridden off to Fort Richardson to alert the blue-coats. Papa swung from his horse, handed the reins to Horace, who led the weary horses toward the corral.

"They weren't there," Papa said when he reached the board and batten shop.

"What?" Jake and I sang out at the same time.

Papa glared, but he knew we had not been joking about such a thing. He cursed savagely, spit, and sucked in a deep breath. "Moses," he said, "found some tracks. Unshod ponies. Indians must have come along, looking for her and the . . . Found them." He cursed once more, only softer this time.

That's when the door opened, and Mama called out: "Supper's ready!"

"Not a word to her," Papa said. "Not one word."

No one ever spoke of the killings—except once briefly—and maybe that's why she haunts me still. To this day, I still dream about her and her newborn. Nightmares send me sitting upright in bed, screaming.

She, the young Kiowa woman who had come into a patch of woods by the creek to give birth to her son . . . and her son, the boy who had been . . . I cannot put it down on paper.

Both were dead when Jake and I had ridden on to the grisly scene. Her throat had been cut, and she had been scalped, and the baby . . .

That's why I have nightmares.

Remembering Charley Conley and the scalp locks hanging on his buckskin shirt, I blamed him.

A week later, a bunch of bluecoats rode into our yard, and Mama and I stepped outside to greet them. Jake was off gallivanting again, paying attention to some local women—neither Mama nor Mrs. Earnhardt would call them ladies. I was reading my geology book. I feared the bluecoats would ask me about the Indian woman and her baby in front of Mama, but the young lieutenant merely removed his hat and bowed.

"Ma'am," he told my mother, "we are chasing a deserter, and if it's not inconvenient would like to water our horses."

"By all means," Mama said.

When I whispered—"Mama, they're Yanks"—she elbowed me in the ribs.

"And, please," Mama told the bluecoats, "fill your canteens."

"We can pay you in script," the shavetail Yankee said.

"You will do no such thing."

Mama even gave them the lemon cookies she had made that morning. They ate them all. I had no dessert that day.

Two days later, when Jake had wandered off again, and I was pushing through some thickets looking for strays, Uncle Moses Gage rode up.

Happy to see anyone, I smiled and pointed at the mule that trailed his horse. "I hope that's a deer that you got wrapped up in that tarp, there," I said. "I'm hungry enough to eat a whole hind-quarter."

"Didn't see your pa at the house," he said.

"No, sir," I said. "And Mama's off visiting Missus Earnhardt."

"Jake?"

I shrugged. "No telling."

He looked over his shoulder, took off his hat, rubbed the close-cropped gray hair atop his head, and returned his hat. "Ride with me, Top Soldier. I feel like comp'ny this day."

"Where you going?"

"Fort Richardson."

That did not tempt me. "What on earth for?" I asked.

He spit. "Think I found their deserter."

"Gonna be a bad spring, Top Soldier," Uncle Moses said. "Bad. Real bad."

That was all he said for the rest of the journey. I kept my hand resting on the grip of the Dragoon, as Uncle Moses's eyes darted in all directions. We hoped, prayed, that we would see no one on the ride up Lost Creek, specifically no Indian.

By fate, coincidence, or God's will, we arrived at the post just a short while after that shavetail of a lieutenant had returned with his patrol. He stepped out of the commanding officer's quarters as we rode up.

In town, church bells began sounding.

"It's Sunday," Uncle Moses told me.

The lieutenant stepped off the porch. He was not happy. "What do you want?" he asked. He was speaking to me, a white boy, and not Moses Gage.

I swallowed down the acid rising in my throat.

"We think we found your deserter, sir." I nodded back at the mule.

The major and others came out as four troopers pulled the body off the mule and laid the load gently on the porch. I stepped back, and turned away, thinking of the Indian girl and her murdered baby.

"Is that him?" I heard the major ask a trooper as he pulled back the tarp.

The young lieutenant spit. With my back to him, I thought he was merely spitting out the terrible taste left in his mouth.

"Mister Cox!" the major roared.

"Begging your pardon, Major," the lieutenant

said, "but that yellow scum deserved this. But that . . . that . . ."

"As you were, Lieutenant. Sergeant, take the corpse to the hospital. Have the surgeon examine him, and report back to me. You two civilians . . ."

I turned around, and thankfully the troopers had covered the dead man again.

The major asked Uncle Moses and me a few questions—meaning Uncle Moses—like where the body had been discovered, things like that. He sighed, then ordered one of the officers to form a detail and ride to the location Moses Gage had given.

While we waited, he asked us where we lived, how long we had been in the area, and if we knew most of the people in town.

"Not most of them," I said, reminding the dumb bluebelly that I lived on a ranch.

"Well, you might be able to help us, anyway," the major said. He turned back to the green lieutenant. "Mister Cox," he said, "escort these two to the morgue. Maybe they can . . ." Instead of finishing, he sighed and walked back into his quarters.

So we followed the detail to the post hospital, but instead of going in, we walked behind the building, past a bunch of prickly pear, and to a small, stone building with a pitched roof, one big window in the side wall, and a recessed door in the front.

Opening the door, Lieutenant Cox motioned us inside. Despite the window and the open door, it was dark inside. But it was the bad smell I didn't think I would ever get out of my nostrils.

"Like I told Major Mallory," Cox said to us. "Newton got what he deserved. Running off. Quitting. But . . ."

I saw the table and the body lying on top of it, covered with a dark woolen blanket.

"That's why I spit in the corporal's face." Lieutenant Cox gestured at the corpse behind him. "He deserved everything those red butchers did to him. But her . . ." He took a few steps backward and reached out to remove the blanket. "The major hopes you might be able to identify this poor creature," the lieutenant explained. "Any help you can be would make things easier. . . ."

The Yankee had barely drawn back the blanket before I turned away and staggered out of the morgue. I didn't have to see the dead, butchered body of Nancy Livermore, a girl I had known. The last time I had seen her, she had been riding in a buggy through Jacksboro with Corporal Newton. She had stuck out her tongue at me. Damn Corporal Newton!

"Yes, sir," I heard Moses Gage saying as I stepped out of the dim light of the morgue and into the bright, blinding sun, fell to my knees, and vomited.

"That's Miss Nancy." Uncle Moses's words echoed inside the stone building. I felt freezing cold. "Lord have mercy. That's Miss Nancy Livermore."

CHAPTER NINETEEN

The days continued to grow warmer, and longer, and the grass grew higher and higher. Wet winters meant green springs, which meant fatter cattle. That made Papa happy, yet the pleasant weather also gave us cause for alarm. Before long we began to hear word of Indian raids, mostly Comanches and Kiowas, across northwestern Texas. Uncle Moses started staying in the bunkhouse with Horace and Jake, whenever he was around.

One late March morning, Charley Conley rode into our yard with a group of about a dozen Rangers. I happened to be on the roof with Horace and Uncle Moses, as we were covering our wooden shingles with layers and layers of dirt, a chore I did not understand at the time. As I've mentioned before, our roof did not leak.

Welcoming the relief from the grueling work, we stood, balancing on the pitched roof, shovels in our hands, as Charley gave us a casual nod, then a curt nod when Mama stepped out onto the porch.

"'Afternoon, Charles," I heard Mama say.

"Ma'am. Mister Braden around?"

"He rode over to Ben Earnhardt's this morning."

"How 'bout Jake?"

"He went to Jacksboro last night. Hasn't come home."

"Uhn-huh." Charley slapped the dust off his hat before returning it to his head. Tugging on his reins, he backed up his pinto and looked up at us.

"Baxter place got hit last night," he said. "Comanch'. Kilt a bull out of spite, run off with four horses and an ass."

"Renee and Matthew all right?" Mama asked from the doorway.

"Scairt outta a year of life, I reckon. Barn was burnt."

"Ridin' after 'em?" Moses asked.

"Reckon so. Our job. Hoped Mister Braden might come along, but he ain't here."

Moses Gage slid over to the ladder, and stepped down, saying: "Let me saddle my hoss, Mister Charley, fetch my Spencer, and I'll ride with you a spell."

"I can go, too!" I called out.

Charley snorted and spit, and Mama said: "Pierce. You'll stay here."

That carved an angry frown on my face, and my lips tightened, even as Uncle Moses looked up at me, saying: "Best stay close, Top Soldier. Stay close." He gave a nod at Horace, some unspoken order, which I figured meant for our hired hand to take care of Mama and me. I would soon be fourteen years old, and I figured I could take care of myself.

Charley Conley rode closer, biting off a large chunk from his tobacco twist. I studied him hard, holding my breath.

After Uncle Moses had gathered up his war bag, Walker Colt, Spencer repeater, and horse, the Rangers loped out of our yard. Turning to Horace, I waited until I heard the door close, meaning Mama was inside.

"Did you see Charley's shirt?" I asked.

"Sure, Top Soldier. I seen 'im. And his shirt. Same smelly buckskin he's had ever since I've knowed him. What of it?"

"There's a new scalp on it."

"Good for Charley." Horace stood, and walked back to the mound of dirt we had shoveled onto the roof to spread out. "Best get back to work."

Horace Butler, I decided, was dumber than everyone else around me, because when you're practically fourteen years old, every adult is dumber than you are. I had seen that new scalp, and I couldn't help but think of the Kiowa woman Jake and I had found beside her dead baby. Charley Conley, I told Jake when he rode up around dusk, had killed the Indian girl and her baby. I had always thought so. Now I had seen the proof.

Jake merely shrugged. His eyes looked redder than usual, and he kept massaging his temples. He had no interest in anything I had to say, and did not join us for supper. I didn't care. I knew I was right. But I wasn't.

"Wil!"

Papa stumbled into the house well past sundown. Mama had been worried sick, fearing the worst after Charley Conley had brought word of the Baxter attack, although she had tried to put on a brave front.

He wore no hat, his lower lip had been bleeding, and a shiner had already begun to form over his right eye. Mama bolted from the chair, and I dropped my geology book, and we both hurried to him.

"I'm all right," he said as he put his right arm around Mama. "Put up my horse, will you, Top Soldier?"

"Yes, Papa." I stepped onto the porch, letting my eyes adjust to the darkness before taking his horse, loose-reined, the saddle slightly off-center.

"What happened?" I heard Mama ask.

"Ben Earnhardt," Papa replied.

That made me curious about how my father had gotten into a row with Captain Earnhardt. Because I wondered who had won the fight, I took care of Papa's horse and traps faster than a seasoned liveryman could have done the job. When

I returned, Mama was dabbing Papa's split lip with a washcloth as Papa leaned back in his chair with a thin slab of beef over his blackening eye.

"Where's Jake?" Papa asked when Mama turned to rinse the washcloth.

"Bunkhouse," I said.

"He didn't eat supper," Mama said as she began to wipe blood and dirt off his mustache. "Horace said he was sick, but didn't want me to look after him."

"Uhn-huh. Too much whiskey, I warrant. Moses?"

"He rode out with Charles Conley," Mama said, and then informed him about the attack on the Baxter place.

"I know. Saw Matthew at Ben's. More of his doings," Papa said.

"Whose doings?" Mama said.

Papa sat up, and removed the beef from his face. "Ben Earnhardt killed that Kiowa in the thicket. And her kid."

I sucked in a deep breath.

"What Kiowa?" Mama asked, her eyes beginning to blaze.

Papa swore underneath his breath, remembering too late that Mama wasn't to know about what Jake and I had found by the creek. Now, he spoke generally about the dead Indian girl and her infant, but he did not mention who had found the bodies. Then he repeated that Captain Earnhardt had killed both of them.

"I don't believe it," Mama said.

"He's been sick ever since Clarke married Janet Conley," Papa said. "Said no son of his would marry some concubine who'd been soiled by Indians. Killing a brave's one thing, but murdering a girl . . . by thunder, she wasn't much older than Pierce here . . . and bashing the newborn's . . ." He stopped suddenly. "I'd like a whiskey, Martha."

"Pierce," Mama said, and I fetched the jug.

Papa told us the story. As he rode up to the Circle E, he saw the captain showing off a scalp to Matthew Baxter, bragging that he had killed some Kiowa wench and her son. "On my range," Papa hissed.

Shoving the scalp in his back pocket, Ben Earnhardt had turned. "What of it?" he asked. "You think Matthew, here, minds, after what them savages done at his place yesterday?"

"You killed a girl. And a baby," Papa said.

"I kilt a squaw. And a nit."

"And left them on my range. Which borders with Matthew's."

"You sayin' I brung these redskin troubles on the Baxters?"

"That's exactly what I'm saying," Papa had told him, and stepped down off his horse.

Yet, to my disgust, Papa explained that before anyone could throw a punch or draw a pistol,

Hog Clagett and Ellis Morrell had stepped in. Oh, Papa and the captain kept shouting insults at one another, but Papa rode off without leaving Captain Earnhardt bleeding or hurting. To my way of thinking, he had ridden off a coward. Again.

"But . . . ?" Mama stepped back, and Papa laughed.

"Put too much spurs to Nicodemus. He stumbled, sent me flying over his neck." He took a pull from the jug, grimacing as the liquor burned his lips. "Lucky he didn't run off, leave me afoot."

Although no punches had been thrown at the Circle E Ranch, the damage had been done. Papa and Captain Earnhardt were feuding, and most of Jack County would wind up backing the captain.

March blew out, and April roared in hot. Our ranch had never been the most popular place in Jack County, but since Papa's squabble with Captain Earnhardt, it seemed as if no one rode up to our place any more. Even Jake stopped riding into town to visit his various ladies, after he came home with a split lip, too, and skinned knuckles.

Mr. Livermore had refused to draw Jake a beer, saying he was part of the "Kiowa-lovin' Braden clan." Jake had pummeled him, before loping out of town ahead of the town marshal. I guess we Bradens had worn out our welcome.

My fourteenth birthday passed with cake and cookies, but no one to wish me well except my family and Horace Butler. The full moon arrived on the 15th, and, a day or two later, Uncle Moses rode up.

"Glad to see you, Moses," Papa said.

The big man shook hands, and gestured with his carbine at the bunkhouse. "Figured I might stay on a spell, iffen it's all right with you, Mister Wil."

"Be proud to have you here," Papa said.

I was happy to have him here, too, for I had feared he had felt as the rest of our neighbors, and that he had turned his back on my family and me.

The next morning, we had more visitors, but these I did not care to see.

Captain Earnhardt rode up with more than two dozen men, most of them Rangers I had seen before, riding with Charley Conley.

"Wil." The captain did not dismount.

"Ben." Papa kept his Winchester Yellow Boy in his hands.

By the corral near the barn, Jake stood, his hands near the two Navy .36-caliber pistols at his waist.

"Injun trouble, Wil," Earnhardt said. He spoke stiffly, uncomfortably, like he had been forced to ask for help from a man he did not like.

Papa said nothing.

"They massacred the Baxters."

Now Papa stepped from underneath the porch, and the captain moved his right hand toward the pistol he wore holstered on his hip.

"Renée?" That came from Mama, standing in the doorway, wringing a towel in her hands.

Hog Clagett, on a sorrel right beside the captain, drew a long breath, and slowly shook his head.

Mama's head dropped. So did the towel.

"Where's Charley Conley?" Papa asked suddenly.

"That's the thing of it, Wil." This time it was Ellis Morrell speaking. "They kilt him, too. I found him . . . scalped, hacked to pieces . . . on the road to Fort Belknap."

"That's nowheres near your place, Wil," Captain Earnhardt said. "Or Matthew Baxter's."

I knew what the captain meant. So did Papa.

Hog Clagett cleared his throat and said: "Shapin' up to be a full uprisin', Wil. Comanch', Kiowa, Cheyenne. All ridin' together."

"Does the Army know?" Papa asked.

That caused Captain Earnhardt to spit out tobacco juice, and wipe his mouth with the back of a faded yellow gauntlet. "Bluebellies? They could not catch a fly with honey, let alone renegade redskins. We saw nothin' but their yellow backs durin' our four years with General Hood."

Papa kept quiet. I had heard enough stories from Horace and Jake to know that the captain's comment was nothing but a Texas lie.

"Wil," Captain Earnhardt said, "we must put our differences aside. This is about all of us. It's about Texas. We need you." He tried to grin, for old time's sake. "And that ol' Enfield rifle you stole from me."

I could remember vaguely the times before the war when Captain Earnhardt would ride up to our place with similar requests. I remembered how proud I was that my father was an Indian fighter, even if, to my knowledge, he had never actually fought Indians. Now Papa looked at me and then back at Mama. He lowered the Winchester, and slowly shook his head.

"Ben," he said, "I think I'd better stay close."

I felt as if I'd been kicked in the stomach. I grit my teeth as I saw the shock of Papa's reply registering on the faces of men I had known, and liked—Hog Clagett and Ellis Morrell and others I was not certain of, at least, not any more.

"Captain." Jake stepped away from the corral and strode across the yard. "Wil here's concerned about Martha, being in the family way and all." It took a couple of days for me to realize the meaning of what Jack had said. Mama was going to have a baby. At the time it was said, I only felt more contempt for my father. "But I'd be right proud to ride with you. Moses, Horace"—he nodded at both men—"I'll be seeing you-all. Top Soldier"—he grinned at me—"help me saddle my horse, will you?"

At least, Jake hadn't been so low, I thought as I scuffed my feet into the barn behind my uncle.

He had done his best to remove another stain Papa had just put on the Braden name.

I grabbed the saddle and blanket while Jake led his horse from the stall. Anger began to seethe in my stomach. My hands shook after I had set the rig on the back of Jake's horse.

"Top Soldier," Jake said, "best watch after Martha and Wil. Comanch' been known to hit a place, steal some stock, ride north toward the Red to pull menfolk away. Then come back to lift hair."

He tightened the cinch, tossed a canteen over the horn, and put his hand on my shoulder.

I could hold back no longer. Looking up, I spat out: "Papa ain't nothing but a coward."

The blow catapulted me into the hay. Jake Braden punched harder than Charley Conley or Bobby Ray Pirkle. Despite the taste of blood in my mouth, I could see my uncle hovering over me, his face masked with rage.

"Boy," he said, "if you grow up to be half the man Wil Braden is, you'll be better than most. Best respect him, learn as much as you can from him . . . while you have the chance."

With that, Jake left me in the hay. I heard the hoof beats as the riders loped off to the north. I sat there feeling sorry for myself. After about ten minutes Horace Butler called out my name. I rose, brushed the hay off my clothes, and waited for Horace to find me.

"Oh, there you are," Horace said, upon seeing me once he entered the barn. "Your pa says you need to run the horses into the barn. Put the chickens in here, too." He grabbed his saddle and bridle, and started toward the corral.

"Where are you going?" I asked.

"Fort Richardson. Wil told me to let the Army know what's goin' on," he answered as he shoved Moses Gage's Sharps rifle into the scabbard.

I shook my head. Papa was turning to the Yankees for help, once again fueling my belief that he had lost his nerve. Maybe it had happened at Sharpsburg. Maybe even long before that. It occurred to me that Papa had only joined Hood's boys because Jake had written to him. A few weeks ago, Papa would not even throw a punch at Captain Earnhardt. I felt certain he had waited to step down off Nicodemus until he knew someone would stop the fight before it even started. At least Jake had whipped Mr. Livermore . . . well, he claimed he had.

Once I had the horses, the chickens, and the rooster in the barn and barred the door, I walked with heavy feet to the house, not paying much attention to anything.

The door opened, and Papa stepped outside. He leaned his Winchester against the wall, and waited as I slowly approached. I noticed the Leech & Rigdon belted in his waistband.

"Where's the Dragoon?" he asked.

I had to remember. "Bunkhouse," I said. "Jake was cleaning it."

"Get it."

Horace Butler was loping away as I raced to the bunkhouse, found the big horse pistol, and came back toward our house. Smoke rose from the chimney, although this day had turned into a scorcher, and Mama had been cooking outside.

I stopped in front of Papa, ashamed to look him in the eye.

"Best get inside," Papa said, and picked up the Winchester and walked toward Lost Creek.

CHAPTER TWENTY

Door shut, window shuttered, a fire in the fireplace with a kettle sitting atop the flames, melting lead bars. Never had I seen anything like this. Sweating, I sat at the table with Mama as we molded balls. Until that moment, I realized, I had never known fear. Not real fear. Now I could taste it.

"Mister Wil's been seein' Indian sign," Uncle Moses said. "So've I. Been a raidin' moon, but don't you-all two fret. We'll send 'em bucks back across the Red with a right smart."

Uncle Moses finished loading his Spencer, and leaned it by the porthole near the door. Next, he took my Dragoon, filled the empty chamber with powder and ball, and set a percussion cap on the nipple. Holstered on his hip, that Walker Colt looked huge, and I saw Papa's Enfield and a double-barrel shotgun nearby. And we still had that Mississippi rifle and the .32-caliber Whitney revolver.

"Papa . . . ," I whispered to Mama, "he used to send us to town. . . ."

I wanted to be anywhere but here. Maybe *I* was the coward.

"Hush," Mama said, but soon her mood softened. She took my hand in hers and whispered: "We're safer here than on the trail to Jacksboro." Tears were forming in her eyes.

I summoned up a manly voice, or tried to. "It'll be all right, Mama."

" 'Course it will," Uncle Moses said.

The worst part might have been the heat. My shirt stuck to my back, and my bandanna turned damp from wiping sweat off my forehead, yet we dared not open the door or window. Now I knew why Papa had made us shovel dirt on our rooftop. Those shingles were made of wood, and wood burned.

Maybe, I thought, *the Indians won't come. God,* I prayed, *don't let . . .*

Papa's Winchester barked outside, once, twice, three times, and Moses Gage picked up the Enfield and hurried to the door, which he swung open. Mama reached for me, but I eluded her

271

grasp, grabbing the Dragoon pistol, and dropping to a knee.

The rifle roared in Uncle Moses's hands, and I drew in a deep breath. My ears rang from the deafening report of the powerful Enfield, but I could still make out the thundering of hoofs and the yipping of Indians. I could see the dust, and Papa running toward the house. He stopped once, turned, fired, jacked another round into the Winchester, and began sprinting again.

"Hurry, Mister Wil!" Moses Gage leaned the smoking Enfield against the wall, drew his Walker Colt, and began firing round after round.

Once Papa reached the porch, he dived through the open doorway as Uncle Moses stepped aside. Before Uncle Moses could close the thick door, however, an arrow whistled through the doorway and stuck, quivering, in Mama's piano. Another slammed against the fireplace, shattering, one part flying back toward Papa's chair, the other landing on the *crinoid*—the fossil I had found, the one Mama said reminded her of a palm tree—on the hearth.

Instantly on his feet, Papa helped Uncle Moses bar the door. Bullets and arrows pelted the house. Papa went to the window, pulled open the shutter, and broke out the panes that had not already been shattered. Uncle Moses holstered the big Walker, picked up the Spencer, and stuck the barrel through the porthole.

Within moments, we were choking on the smoke from our weapons, which only intensified the heat.

"Top Soldier!" Papa beckoned me over. "Stay low."

Leaving the heavy Dragoon, still unfired, on the floor, I crawled over the floor to Papa, where he handed me his Winchester, the barrel burning hot to the touch, and said through the smoke: "Reload. But keep down." He pulled the revolver from his waistband, and stuck the Leech & Rigdon out the window.

So it went. Mama managed to crawl over to Uncle Moses, to reload weapons for him, while I did the same for Papa's Winchester and his revolver. The Yellow Boy and Spencer, firing copper rimfire cartridges, were much easier than reloading the Enfield, the Mississippi rifle, the shotgun, or any of our cap-and-ball revolvers. I had never realized how much of an arsenal we had, maybe not even why.

Papa had built the house with such an attack in mind, for the Indians could not reach the barn door or corral without being caught in Papa's or Uncle Moses's gunsights. But even though those Kiowas, Comanches, or maybe even Cheyennes, did not care for our horses, they took them before the night was over, along with our chickens and the rooster. No, this was a murder raid.

To avenge the dead Kiowa girl and her newborn.

Smoke continued to sting our eyes, and powder and sweat blackened our faces and hands. My throat felt as though it was coated with sand, my tongue felt heavy, my lips chapped. I handed Papa the Winchester.

"Papa." I flinched as an arrow thudded against the wall past the shutter. Papa shot a glance at me. "That's the last of the cartridges for the Winchester," I told him.

His head bobbed, but he said nothing. Concentrating outside, he levered a round into the chamber, and waited to fire.

"Regroupin'," Uncle Moses said.

"Yeah," Papa confirmed.

Mama leaned against the wall, her face pale. "How long . . . ," she started to ask but paused. Then: "Till . . . Horace . . . could bring back . . . ?" But she did not finish.

And no one answered because no one knew if Horace Butler had even made it to Fort Richardson. He could be lying dead along Lost Creek.

Suddenly Mama just slid down the wall, falling on her side.

Uncle Moses cried out, and I hurried to her. Papa, mouth taut, and Moses Gage stayed where they were, ready for the next attack.

Having just fainted, Mama came to and began protesting, though quite weakly, as I helped her move over, easing her onto a rug behind the piano that I had once said resembled "a fat man's coffin." My joke no longer seemed so funny, especially after I broke off the arrow stuck in the piano's center. I hurried to fetch our chaps and coats, and then made something of a pillow for Mama's head.

"I'm all right," Mama said as she settled down.

"You just stay there, Missus Braden!" Uncle Moses called from the porthole.

"I have to . . ."

"Stay put."

Papa's Winchester roared.

I reloaded long guns for Papa and Uncle Moses, and brought the revolvers to Mama, who demanded that she could load those while still sitting behind the Steinway. No one objected. We really needed her help, too, if we wanted to survive.

"They've set the hay afire," Moses Gage said. "Think a bunch of 'em be behind the barn, gettin' to our horses."

"That won't satisfy them," Papa said.

"I knows it. Just a shame is all. You gots good horses."

"Thanks to you."

Moses Gage grinned. "Yeah," he said. "That's right."

When the Indians drew back again, Papa asked for water. Mama tried to stand, but was too weak, so I hurried to the kitchen, grabbed a canteen, and brought it to Papa first, Uncle Moses next, and then Mama. I took a healthy swallow myself, as I heard the crescendo of the war whoops and shooting as the Indians came at us.

By then, the Winchester Yellow Boy lay on the floor, next to the empty Spencer. Papa had turned to the Mississippi rifle, the Whitney, and his Leech & Rigdon. Uncle Moses had his Walker, Papa's battered Enfield, and the shotgun. For some reason, maybe because I had left it on the floor and no one had had time to think about it, the old Dragoon lay on the floor, still unfired. Or perhaps Papa and Uncle Moses were just leaving it loaded, in case the raiders got inside our house. You know . . . *saving that last bullet.*

This attack seemed to be waning quickly, but, just before the braves withdrew, I heard a deafening roar, followed by a scream.

With a curse, Papa fired his revolver in rapid succession, withdrew from the window, slamming the shutter closed. He did not take the time to bolt it, before hurrying over to Uncle Moses. I reached him first.

Light and dust showed through a gaping, fist-size hole in the thick door, and Uncle Moses sat among the empty cartridges that littered the floor. He pressed both hands against his stomach. Blood streamed between his fingers, puddling around him.

"Lord A'mighty, Mister Wil," he said. "I'm kilt."

"Hush up, Moses. You've nicked yourself worse . . . ," Papa began, but couldn't finish, knowing he couldn't help Moses Gage.

While our attention was on Uncle Moses, an Indian had pushed open the shutter and started climbing inside. At the same time a gun barrel showed through the hole in the door. Papa whirled, snapped a shot from the Leech & Rigdon, but the weapon, hot and fouled from so much shooting, misfired. Shifting the revolver into his hand like a club, he ran toward the Indian climbing through the window.

"Top Soldier!" Moses called. "Look out."

I grabbed the barrel sticking through the hole in the door just as the old weapon discharged. The ball whined as it ricocheted off the chimney, and slammed into the piano. The heat from the barrel burned my hand, but I continued to yank it until suddenly the barrel jerked back out of my hand, propelling me against the door. I let go, and the weapon disappeared. The door shuddered. Behind it, came the grunts and the cries of the warriors as they tried to push their way inside. To kill us all.

The next thing I knew Papa was kneeling beside me, sticking the Whitney's barrel through the hole and pulling the trigger as quickly as he could cock the hammer. Immediately dropping the empty .32, he grabbed Uncle Moses's Walker, then stuck its barrel through the hole, and fired the big .44 twice. Shrieks sounded as the warriors withdrew, and Papa moved back to the window, snapping a final shot with the shotgun.

I saw the Indian who had been trying to get inside through the window. He lay on the floor, his head a bloody pulp.

Papa started to pull the shutter closed again, when he stopped. "That crazy fool!" he yelled, and hurried to the door.

I watched, terrified, as Papa hurled off the bar, pulled open the door, and charged outside, armed with only the double-barrel shotgun—and it held only one round now.

"Wil!" Mama screamed.

That's when I heard the Rebel yell.

I remembered it from the evening when Uncle Jake and Captain Earnhardt's men had cut loose with those cries. But in the house, after supper, while Jake told stories . . . that was one thing. Hearing it in an actual battle . . . well, that felt completely different. Even after an hour of Indian shouts and whoops, this yell made me shiver.

Turning to Uncle Moses, I sucked in a deep breath. I knew he was dead, but tears would have to wait.

The door to our house wide open, Papa stood outside with only a shotgun. I snatched the unfired Dragoon, and leaped over Moses Gage's legs, staggering through the door, out past the porch.

"Pierce!" Mama cried out.

I saw Uncle Jake Braden galloping his lathered horse into our yard, pursued by three Indians. I knew there were others out there, in the woods along the creek, behind the barn, the bunkhouse, the board and batten shop, everywhere, firing rifles and arrows. Jake's horse went down, and my uncle kicked free of the stirrups, tumbling head over heels in the dust.

Papa's shotgun roared. An Indian's horse dropped, temporarily pinning its rider. Tossing the empty shotgun aside, Papa ran to help his younger brother.

Indians had us in what Horace Butler had once called an enfilade. There was no way Papa, Jake, or I should have survived. But, recalling Jake's stories, he and Papa never should have lived through Sharpsburg.

Stepping into the yard, I cocked the massive .44, brought it up, and squeezed the trigger. The recoil landed me on my backside, and I sat there, watching Papa grab Jake, pull him to his feet, usher him toward our house.

Behind him, and on all of our sides, the Indians were charging right behind us.

Struggling, I tried to cock the Dragoon again, as Papa shoved Jake past me with one hand. His left hand grabbed my collar, and he dragged me inside the house, too. The three of us fell over the lifeless body of Moses Gage, but it was Papa who reacted quickly. He came to his feet, knocked one Indian aside, sent him crashing against Mama's piano. Then he snatched up the Enfield, fired from his hip, ducked underneath a lance thrust from a warrior in the doorway, swung the heavy rifle, and crushed the skull of that warrior. Wordlessly the brave fell onto the floor beside Moses Gage. Next Papa hurled the empty rifle through the door. The flying Enfield knocked another warrior to the ground. Three others nearly tripped over their fallen comrade.

That gave Papa just enough time to fetch the Navy Colt Jake had dropped. He slammed the door shut, dropped to the floor, and stuck the revolver barrel through the hole in the door. He squeezed the trigger till the Colt clicked empty.

At Mama's scream, I turned to see that the Indian who'd been knocked unconscious had come to and had my mother by her hair, a tomahawk in his right hand.

Papa hurled the empty Navy at the brave, who ducked and laughed as his eyes locked on me. He let go of my mother's hair and threw the tomahawk, which sailed just over my head.

The Dragoon roared, sending me sliding across the floor and dropping the Indian to the floor.

At the same time, Jake, having gotten his wind back, drew his other Navy and moved toward the porthole by the front door while Papa eased the smoking Dragoon from my hand and returned to the window.

A scattering of pistol shots echoed outside, followed by an eerie silence.

"Rangers are on their way," Jake said after the longest while. His chest heaved. He bled from both nostrils, his lip, and scratches on his face. His shirt was ripped. "Just need to hold them off a few minutes more."

With Nutmeg, Nicodemus, all of our horses, and even our chickens, the Indians retreated to Red River, carrying with them their wounded and dead, except the warriors slain inside our cabin. Five minutes later, Captain Earnhardt and the Rangers galloped into our yard, staying only briefly, before riding off in an effort to punish the raiders.

Within the hour, Horace Butler showed up with a bunch of bluecoats from Fort Richardson, led by Lieutenant Cox.

What became known in Jack County as the Rafter B fight had ended.

EPILOGUE

In 1871 and 1873, I rode up the Chisholm Trail with Papa, satisfying my curiosity about Abilene and Ellsworth, yet I was no cowboy, and certainly not much of a rancher. Papa knew that, which is why Beth, my kid sister, got the ranch. She still has it, and has run it with her own family for the past four years. Me? Well, the fall after the Rafter B fight, Papa allowed me to return to Miss Riley's school. She continued to nurture my fascination with rocks, fossils, geology. When I turned eighteen, she helped me get accepted into Colorado's Territorial School of Mines in Golden. That led me to various ventures in Colorado and New Mexico until the Paulton Coal Mining Company offered me a job here in Pennsylvania that I could not turn down.

Twice more, in 1871, Captain Earnhardt rode to our house, asking Papa to fetch the old Enfield he had stolen from him, and ride after Comanches and Kiowas. Of course, Papa rode with the captain, but they never caught any Indians. Ben Earnhardt went on to serve in the Texas legisla-ture. He remained neighborly with Papa, but I wouldn't call it friendly. He dropped dead of a heart attack in 1885 and is buried alongside many other state dignitaries and Confederate veterans in an Austin cemetery.

Horace Butler parted ways with us after the 1871 drive to Abilene, said he wanted to drift west, and we never heard from him again.

After Grandfather J.J. Braden died the following winter, Uncle Jake returned to Harrisburg. Jake's wild streak faded, and he became a respectable member of society in South Texas. He's still there, ancient, stove-up, and, with a mouth full of dentures, unable to recreate that fabled Rebel yell.

These days, folks in northwestern Texas are more likely to bring up Britt Johnson, another Negro who was killed by Indians in 1871, and a more storied Indian attack at Salt Creek, also in 1871, when telling windies about those wild days in Texas. Even old-timers in Jack County rarely brag about Uncle Moses, who was buried a hero and mourned by many back in 1870.

By 1875, the Comanches and Kiowas were pinned up on the reservation north of the Red River. Jack County became peaceful. The Army abandoned Fort Richardson in 1878.

So Papa and Mama lived out their days at our ranch, and now rest peacefully near Lost Creek, alongside five other graves: another sister, after Beth, who lived just six months, Moses Gage, and the three Indians killed in that attack on that April day in 1870.

My sister, who was born that October, always says I'm guilty of some Texas stretcher when I relate the story of the attack on our cabin, but she hadn't been born yet and has never experienced an Indian raid.

People ask me how many Indians we killed. I have no idea. Three for certain. Papa killed two of those. I shot the other.

The one I killed still haunts me.

His face was painted, his eyes wide open, his braids wrapped in otter skins. He was barely older than me. How well I remembered him. He was the Kiowa who had traded a knife and sheath for a copy of *Peter Parley's Wonders of the Earth, Sea, and Sky.* Uncle Moses had told me that the Indian would "just rip that book apart, stuff it in the next shield he makes. Won't stop a bullet. . . ." Well, it wouldn't have the chance.

Mostly, though, I remember Papa, especially those last few minutes before Captain Earnhardt and the Rangers rode into our yard.

With Jake standing guard by the porthole, Mama on the floor, shaking, and me just sitting there, stunned, Papa was busy. He covered Moses Gage's body with a greatcoat, checked on Mama, and began reloading what weapons we had while protecting us.

That's when I started crying, and could not control the flood.

After a quick glance outside, Papa shoved the

Dragoon into his waistband. He crossed the floor, kneeled down next to me, and pulled me close.

I wasn't crying because I had killed a man, or because I was scared, or even for Uncle Moses. Those tears flowed because I felt ashamed of everything I had said, and felt, about my father.

As Papa held me in his arms, I sobbed even harder. He kissed the top of my head, and in a cabin that smelled of gunsmoke, of blood, of death, I felt safe in his arms, overcome by his love.

"It's all right, Pierce," Papa whispered. "Let them flow, Son. Even a top soldier cries."

ABOUT THE AUTHOR

Johnny D. Boggs has worked cattle, shot rapids in a canoe, hiked across mountains and deserts, traipsed around ghost towns, and spent hours poring over microfilm in library archives—all in the name of finding a good story. He's also one of the few Western writers to have won six Spur Awards from Western Writers of America (for his novels, *Camp Ford*, in 2006, *Doubtful Cañon*, in 2008, and *Hard Winter* in 2010, *Legacy of a Lawman*, *West Texas Kill*, both in 2012, and his short story, "A Piano at Dead Man's Crossing," in 2002) as well as the Western Heritage Wrangler Award from the National Cowboy and Western Heritage Museum (for his novel, *Spark on the Prairie: The Trial of the Kiowa Chiefs*, in 2004). A native of South Carolina, Boggs spent almost fifteen years in Texas as a journalist at the Dallas *Times Herald* and Fort Worth *Star-Telegram* before moving to New Mexico in 1998 to concentrate full time on his novels. Author of dozens of published short stories, he has also written for more than fifty newspapers and magazines, and is a frequent contributor to *Boys' Life* and *True West*. His Western novels cover a wide range. *The Lonesome Chisholm Trail* (2000) is an authentic cattle-drive story, while *Lonely*

Trumpet (2002) is an historical novel about the first black graduate of West Point. *The Despoilers* (2002) and *Ghost Legion* (2005) are set in the Carolina backcountry during the Revolutionary War. *The Big Fifty* (2003) chronicles the slaughter of buffalo on the southern plains in the 1870s, while *East of the Border* (2004) is a comedy about the theatrical offerings of Buffalo Bill Cody, Wild Bill Hickok, and Texas Jack Omohundro, and *Camp Ford* (2005) tells about a Civil War base-ball game between Union prisoners of war and Confederate guards. "Boggs's narrative voice captures the old-fashioned style of the past," *Publishers Weekly* said, and *Booklist* called him "among the best Western writers at work today." Boggs lives with his wife Lisa and son Jack in Santa Fe. His website is www.johnnydboggs.com.

Center Point Large Print
600 Brooks Road / PO Box 1
Thorndike, ME 04986-0001 USA

(207) 568-3717

US & Canada:
1 800 929-9108
www.centerpointlargeprint.com